The Mystics
of The
Green Heron

VIRGINIA STATE PENITENTIARY

John Jones

Copyright © 2022 by John Jones.

Library of Congress Control Number: 2022916772
ISBN: Hardcover   978-1-6698-4621-5
 Softcover   978-1-6698-4620-8
 eBook   978-1-6698-4619-2

All rights reserved. No part of this book may be reproduced or transmitted in any form or by any means, electronic or mechanical, including photocopying, recording, or by any information storage and retrieval system, without permission in writing from the copyright owner.

This is a work of fiction. Names, characters, places and incidents either are the product of the author's imagination or are used fictitiously, and any resemblance to any actual persons, living or dead, events, or locales is entirely coincidental.

NOTE: THIS BOOK CONTAINS ADULT LANGUAGE.

For information related to the Front Cover Photograph, see Foot Note 1.

Print information available on the last page.

Rev. date: 09/08/2022

To order additional copies of this book, contact:
Xlibris
844-714-8691
www.Xlibris.com
Orders@Xlibris.com
846709

Contents

Dedications v
Preface vii

Chapter 1   The Green Heron Penitentiary 1
Chapter 2   The Green Heron Quarry 8
Chapter 3   The GHVSP Secret Meetings 15
Chapter 4   Avenue Of Escape from The GHVSP 22
Chapter 5   How Are The Planned Vacations Paid For 32
Chapter 6   Will Doug Lentz and Frank Daly Sing 38
Chapter 7   Simple Escape Plans 45
Chapter 8   Simple Escape Plans Fail 51
Chapter 9   On The Run What Next 57
Chapter 10   Ambushed and Murdered 64
Chapter 11   Inside Outside Help 72
Chapter 12   Both GHVSP Escapees Located 80
Chapter 13   Escape Number Two Succeeds 87
Chapter 14   What Happened Where Are They 94
Chapter 15   Eliminate Johnson and James 100
Chapter 16   GHQM Tragedy 107
Chapter 17   Douglas Lentz And Frank Daly Located 113
Chapter 18   The Secret Of The Steel Drums 122
Chapter 19   A Surprise And Shocking Conclusion 128

Foot Notes 137
Glossary 139
About The Author 143

Dedications

To my Beloved Late Wife LaVerne (Susie) Jones whose love and understandings still inspires me to continue to write. Hon, I love and miss you very much.

JOHN

Sentiments

    GOD Never Forgets Us.

Preface

This very Mysterious Story will bring Strange Feelings to your very Soul as you realize what these incarcerated men and women endure each and every day of their life. Most are totally lost souls with little or no hope. The only Salvation they have is the satisfaction they put themselves in this position and are paying the price for their Sins Early.

    The main stages of this Story begin in a newly constructed High Security Penitentiary in the State of Virginia, United States of America (U.S.A.). Named "The Green Heron". All of the prison inmates are hard core Felons with only one main daily thought on their mind, "Escape". After being confined for a very short time they all now realize how precious Freedom can be once it is lost. Many of them seek to escape, but few succeed. The ones that fail face the Ultimate Penalty, a cruel unknown death; A Penitentiary Mystic. Is this new State Penitentiary, the Green Heron escape proof? You must read this Strange Story to find out.

Chapter 1

THE GREEN HERON PENITENTIARY

As you read this strange story it will hold your undivided attention in many ways and keep you thinking about your life long experiences and the way you still approach every day at this time.

This story begins inside the cold stone walls of the Green Heron Virginia State Penitentiary (GHVSP) a.k.a. "The Quarry" located in the State of Virginia, U.S.A. This Penitentiary is located approximately eighty five statue miles West of Richmond, Virginia just off of Virginia State Route (Rt) 250 not far from the small Hamlet of Carrisbrook. As you pass the intersection of Carrisbrook continue on Rt 250 for about another mile there you turn right on to a private now state maintained road named "Lolly Dolly Road".

As you travel down Lolly Dolly Road for about two miles, in the distance you will begin to see the GHVSP. The Penitentiary has the sinister dungeon looking appearance you have read, heard about and expect. This Penitentiary has an evil and cruel reputation and many of the inmates, men and women confined behind these stone walls have never been seen or heard of again for unknown reasons, a Penitentiary Mystic. Also, another Penitentiary Mystic is that many escape attempts have been tried but all are recorded as unsuccessful. Why? "No tickee, No laundry"!

The GHVSP is a typical designed Penitentiary very similar to the old state prison in Richmond located on Spring Street. The GHVSP was constructed on the old abandon Lolly Dolly Family Granite Quarry land in early 1933. It is unique as it is designed in to three separate yet interfaced sections. The West Wing Houses the male inmates, the East Wing Houses the female inmates and the Middle Center Section Houses the Business and Administration Offices. When fully occupied under normal operating conditions it Houses a population of about two hundred total inmates. All of these inmates for the most part are considered career type hard core felons and most are serving life long prison terms with little or no chance for parole.

The GHVSP is completely surrounded by a twenty five feet high wall using granite stone mined from this very Quarry. The wall is designed to contain the usual Armed Security Guard Towers and Flood Light Assemblies. The Wall has two heavy automatic entry Gates. One gate serves the rear and opens to the Quarry Granite Mines and outside Gardens. The other gate serves the front and main entrance and opens up looking straight down Lolly Dolly Road.

The GHVSP holding cells are the usual in size, but for convience, security and safety concerns contain full latrines with showers. All inmates are confined under normal conditions in their holding cell 24/7 except when removed to attend their related work detail duties or exercise breaks. For the most part the work details for the male inmates is working in the mine operations. The female inmates work details for the most part are kitchen police (KP), dining hall, laundry and outside garden duties.

All inmates when outside of their holding cell unless they are prison trustees are restrained in some way. These restraining devices when inside are usually small shackles. Outside a standard anklet ball and chain is used. Prison trustee inmates are unrestrained and roam free. Meals are served once a day and delivered to each holding cell that contains under normal conditions two inmates. This covered food tray is delivered by a prison trustee usually around 0600Hr. The only inmates that eat their meals in the dining hall are the inside workers and prison trustees. The entire GHVSP Staff Members are allowed to eat all meals in the dining hall cafeteria style if they so choose too.

All inmates with behavior problems or trouble makers receive various Automatic Solitary Confinement Sentences (ASCS) with a daily diet of bread and water. Inmates that are constant trouble makers are suddenly lost while attempting to escape. Another Penitentiary Mystic.

Unlike most of the state's confinement institutions' the GHVSP Security Force is well armed at all times inside and out with lock and load shoot to kill orders as issued by Chief Warden Kenneth Foster. This GHVSP Security Force is under command of Captain Charles Stanton, (a.k.a. Charlie). Captain Stanton is a hard ass experienced law enforcement officer that has come up through the ranks the hard way. He is a no nonsense Law officer with a tough cruel reputation and does not take a lot of fuckin bull shit (BS) from anyone including his GHVSP Staff. New arriving guests (Inmates) that try to test him soon find this out the hard way. Rule number one do not fuck or try to pull any shit over on the Captain. He will kick your ass and put your ass under a ASCS in a hurry.

The GHVSP has a standard work force that includes Civil and Private employees. All of these employees are under the strict supervision and answer directly to the Chief Warden Ken Foster (a.k.a. The Chief or Ken). He too is like Captain Stanton and does not put up with a lot of cheap BS. He has earned his position and knows his job. He also has a cruel background and has a very short temper. Behind his back he is called a first class ass hole (AH). Serving directly under him along with Captain Stanton is Assistant Wardens Lieutenants (Lt) Erma Kersay, (a.k.a. Em) Female Wing and Lt Jason Mitchell Male Wing.

Under the very strict leadership of The Chief the GHVSP operates for the most part very well with very little or no problems. All of the employees know their jobs and realize their positions. They also realize they are always working in a dangerous environment and that most of these inmates they oversee daily are serving life time sentences with little or no chance for parole. The only chance they will ever be free and see the outside again is to escape. All these inmates have plans for different avenues of escape. A Penitentiary Mystic, no one ever succeeds. (No One Escapes). No tickee, No laundry!

The GHVSP first opened its gates on April 04, 1933. It was constructed as part of the Great Depression Program by the Civilian Conservation Corps (CCC). (See Foot Notes 2 & 3). It has a known reputation as a "No Escape Facility" a Penitentiary Mystic. Only two inmates thus far have tried to escape; William Lentz and Paul Daly. A Penitentiary Mystic, these two inmates have never been seen or heard of since. Another Penitentiary Mystic, a rumor passed along over the years has it their remains can be found in a steel drum on the bottom of the "Big Lake" located in the Green Heron Quarry Mine (GHQM).

So much for now about the GHVSP and its Mystics. We will speak more about the GHVSP and its Penitentiary Mystics throughout as this strange story unfolds.

January 02, 1936. Thursday morning about 0800Hr an unmarked Virginia State Bureau of Investigation (VSBI) Caged Van (a.k.a. Patty Wagon) drives up to the Main Entrance Gate of the GHVSP. The Tower Guards on duty recognizes the Van but still only opens a small outside box where one of the Van's VSBI Agents gets out and puts in a coded note and sends it up to him. The Guard verifies the names of the Van's occupants on the note. They are, VSBI Agents Tracey Leyden and David Sikes and the two new GHVSP inmate arrivals Douglas Lentz and Frank Daly, both caged and shackled in the rear of the Van. Both of these new inmates are career type criminals and have been convicted of many serious crimes that include drug sales, prostitution, gun running and the worse, first degree murder. Both are serving life time sentences with no chance for parole.

After verification of the VSBI van and its occupants are complete the van is allowed to pass through the Main Gate as it mechanically opens. The van proceeds over to the center section of the GHVSP and parks in front of the Administration and Business office. Security Force Captain Stanton with two assistants walk out to except the two new inmate arrivals. They follow the usual processing procedures that includes the Confinement and Transfer papers. Captain Stanton shakes the two VSBI Agents hands as his two assistants walk the two shackled prisoners away to complete processing. He smiles and says hello Tracey and Dave long time no see, how have you two AH been doing? You guys come on in the office and get a cup of hot coffee and warm up a bit its cold as hell out here. They all laugh as they have been long time friends and worked in the State Law Enforcement System together for years.

Where have you guys been keeping yourselves? Hell, it's been a while, did you have a nice New Year's Eve? Hell, Charlie your wonderful Walldorf Hotel located in this beautiful GOD forbidden "Quarry" does not have a lot of turn over and stays pretty well booked up and occupied plus we only bring you very special screened out clients, as they all laugh out loud at Dave's humorous reply. Dave are you still going with that beautiful lady, Betty Daly we met at the Music Awards Show last year held at the Old Norview Theater in Norfolk? You bet your sweet ass I am! She is my special honey but her AH father is giving us problems. Oh shit, sorry to hear that. Is there anything I can help you with, we go back a long ways? No Charles not really. Everything was going well between us until her father found out she was dating a VSBI Agent then the fuckin wheels came off. Dave, I do not understand that, it looks like her father would be proud of that. Well Charlie her dear devoted father is none other than Mr. Harrison Paul Daly the local Carbone Mafia Cartel "Don" or Boss. He of course works under the control of the notorious Carbone Mafia Cartel Family out of New York City, (NYC) New York (NY). Son of a bitch (SOB) Dave what are you two going to do? If you know all this about his background why don't the Federal Bureau of Investigation (FBI) step in and arrest him I will be more than glad to save him a room up here if need be? Charles this is not funny, this man likes Law Enforcement Officers dead in a drum dumped overboard in the Chesapeake Bay. I know Dave, sorry about the joke.

Dave to answer your question the Feds tell us they have this man under surveillance 24/7 but at his time do not have a strong enough case to bring him down yet. Betty told me her father is a pussy cat until you get on his dark side. When this happens, people go on one way boat rides out on the Chesapeake Bay. SOB Dave what are you and Betty going to do? It's nothing we can do until the FBI or the VSBI build a strong enough case against him and take him down. GOD only knows when that will happen. He has a lot of well known folks on the take and in his pocket. Running off and settling down elsewhere is out of the question as he would have us tracked down and a boat ride out on the Chesapeake Bay in a drum is not the way I want to go. Hell, Charles if you want to add fuel to the fire; that was Betty's kid brother Frank Daly we just dropped off. Not only that her older brother is Paul Daly one of your GHVSP infamous escapees. By the way Charles whatever happen to him? Who knows it's a Penitentiary Mystic?

Well enough about my problems I will keep you posted on the Daly's as the beat goes on. Tracey and I have to get on back to Richmond we still have plenty of work to take care of. Charles this fuckin Law Enforcement work "Sucks". Tell me about it, Dave it never ends. By the way Charles Our New Year's Eve was fuckin great! Tracey and I both worked late, got up early and drove up here. That's another drawback to this fuckin job you are on call 24/7, 365.

Chapter 2

THE GREEN HERON QUARRY

The Green Heron Quarry derives its name from the hundreds of Little Green Heron Birds that now habitat the many small lakes and ponds created by years of Quarry Granite Surface Strip Mining Operations. This Quarry has been opened and in full operation most of this time by the Dolly Family. Over the recent years the demand for Quarry Mine Products have diminished to a level that old man Herman Dolly (a.k.a. Lolly) decided the small profits of this mine were not worth the time and efforts involved; plus, the ever growing enforcement of Federal and State Regulations were beginning to be a burden and he decided to just sell out to any reasonable buyer.

As expected, the Virginia State Bureau of Prisons decided to purchase the now abandon Quarry Complex and its vast surrounding property to use as a later construction site for its newly planned Penitentiary. This proved to be a very satisfactory transaction for the Dolly Family as well as the State of Virginia.

This completely stripped land gave the State a convenient site for its newly planned Penitentiary plus a much needed source of crushed gravel for its ever expanding roadways and other miscellaneous gravel requirements. Not only that the state sad to say has an endless source of labor as provided by convicted inmates now used only to cut roadside grasses and other simple state maintenance projects.

As soon as the state of Virginia took control of this abandon Quarry, it quickly reopened it using convicted inmates that were considered non-dangerous and short timers. These inmates were bused in from other areas daily to do the mine work. Later temporary military type barracks were constructed on the grounds to house these inmates and they stayed over for brief periods. Most of these inmates of course worked the Quarry with little or no problems and for the most part were treated very well. Although the work was considered hard labor most of the inmates were just relieved to get away from inside confinement.

Most of these inmates other than prison trustees when working outside of the barracks were still restrained under state laws in some way usually by anklet ball and chains as escaping was considered easy in this vast opened stripped land. The main Quarry job was to hand crush using heavy manual hammers the larger stripped granite stone in to small size gravel rocks for roadway construction and other building projects.

Sad to say but like so many of the early strip mines throughout the State the land was left opened and laid to waste. The Dolly Family being no different followed suit and left this land stripped and unvegetated. State and Federal Laws now require plowing and replanting all native vegetation to these lands. As the years passed the Quarry continued to operate and serve its main purpose and later as we now know in April 04, 1933 became the site of the now newly constructed dreaded GHVSP a.k.a.

"The Quarry". This Penitentiary sad to say was required as the Virginia State incarceration population is increasing at alarming rates. Why?

As time passes let's move on to March 27,1939. Monday about 0800Hr two of the most notorious inmates within the GHVSP, Doug Lentz and Frank Daly are taken under guard from their holding cell number (No.) 201 to join their assigned Quarry work details. As required, they are shackled ball and chained and marched to the Green Heron Quarry Mine (GHQM). This huge interior mine is a cavern within itself. Well hidden within one of its many branches is a huge deep water lake known as "The Big Lake" that is supplied by the endless Potomac Aquifer. This Mine as far as the GHVSP staff is concerned is named and called the GHQM. As far as the GHVSP inmates are concerned it's called the Main Gate To Hell (MGTH). Their reason for that name is the cruel private contracted outside supervised work within is hot, hard, dirty, dangerous and always cruel. It requires the removal of large heavy dusty blown up pieces of granite stone.

As the day progresses Doug and Frank now on their 1200Hr lunch break are walking along together carrying their steel anklet balls and chain. While slowly walking and chatting Frank ask Doug, well what do you think? Frank I am not sure, we can still continue to plan an escape of some kind but I have still not seen anything that indicates the escape avenue code written in my Carbone Mafia Cartel note. SOB you AH I thought you told me it was a done deal. You AH how long have you had that fuckin note? Frank it was given to me incognito on New Year's Day by an inside guard working in the VSBI Holding Cell Barracks in Richmond just before we were transported up here to the GHVSP. Does the fuckin code state GHQM? Hell no, you dumb shit all it states is "MGTH" and the word "SHE"!!!!!!

Frank, I assume the "MGTH" means this Quarry mine as we all call it the "MGTH". I can buy that but what the fuck does the word "SHE" mean? How the fuck do I know I am still trying to figure that one out. SOB Doug we have been locked up in this fuckin hell hole for about thirty nine months so far. We finally get assigned to this GHQM work detail so we can set up an avenue of escape using the code stated in your fuckin Carbone Mafia Cartel note and you do not know what directions we need to take next. SOB Doug are you sure we are even in the right place? Yes, Frank we are in the right place, all I can tell you at this time is keep looking for clues and thoughts that may tell us what the word "SHE" means.

April 10, 1939. Monday about 1800Hr inmates Doug Lentz and Frank Daly are securely locked back in their holding cell No. 201. Having cleaned up after completing another dirty, dusty, hot and hard day's work in the MGTH Mine Doug is taking a well earned break just reading more of Adolf Hitlers infamous novel "Mein Kampf" (My Struggle)". As he reads, he suddenly stops as he comes to the word "SHE" and finds out Adolf Hitler defines it as an acronym that stands for "Satan & Hells Exit". SOB, Frank I think I may have found a clue to the word "SHE". Are you sure I hope this is not more of your BS? No, here in Adolf Hitlers book I am reading a statement where he writes the word "SHE" and defines it as "Satan & Hells Exit". Hell Doug, that's all well and good but what the hell does it tell us, we are still in the fuckin dark. How does that relate back to the MGTH Mine we work in every day? Frank just maybe the acronym "SHE" and the abbreviation MGTH tie together in some way. Doug, I think you are full of shit and sipping to much "Syrup". Frank, I do not think so, as my Carbone Mafia Cartel note clearly speaks to "MGTH" and "SHE".

Frank just keep looking for more clues and think positive and we will find the answer. We will find a way to escape from this hell hole. Well, if my cousin William Lentz and your brother Paul Daly succeeded in escaping, we will too! Doug did those two guys really escape? GHVSP Records list both of these guys drown in the "Big Lake" while trying to escape. Frank those GHVSP Records contain a lot of Penitentiary Mystics just remember that old buddy.

Hell Doug, just give it up and stop grabbing straws we have a nice place here, HA, HA! Hell, I am beginning to enjoy living here. Hell, where else can you go and get free room and board. Just think we have our own private holding cell, plenty of cold food to eat, a steady job working eight to ten hours a day in a deep hot fuckin granite mine busting cheap ass granite in to small pieces of fuckin rocks. Shit Doug I fuckin "A" love it, HA, HA! Frank, keep your day job, your stand up comedy act sucks. Frank just settle down, let's get a smoke and a short swag of "Syrup" and call it a day. Sounds good to me as the mine rail car picks us up tomorrow around 0800Hr for another wonderful day at the office, HA, HA! Speaking of syrup how do we stand? Our syrup bottle is getting low. I better say something to our prison trustee old Henry Johnson tomorrow when he drops off our food trays so he can bring us another bottle. Do we have enough cash in the till to pay for it? Yes, but old Henry Johnson told me that the AH Chief Warden has raised the price to five dollars per eight ounce "Syrup Bottle". You mean to tell me that bastard raise the price one whole dollar for that snuggled in cheap ass bootlegged whiskey? He sure did not only that he also raised the price on cigarettes to twenty five cents a pack. Damn Doug what the hell does that SOB do with all that money? Old Henry Johnson told me the GHVSP Treasurer/ Certified Public Accountant (T/CPA) James Rawls Junior collects it and puts it in a GHVSP Slush Fund and sends it to the Virginia State Treasures Office every quarter. Hell Doug do you really believe that shit? Hell no, but shit happens when you have the fox guarding the hen house. Could this be another Penitentiary Mystic? Doug, mark my words; if It can be said it can be read, one of these days that no good Chief Warden will get his you just wait and see!!!!!!!!!???????

Doug, do you think we really have any chance of escaping from this fuckin place using a Mafia Cartel escape plan? Not really, Frank the only way we can escape is develop a plan of our own or become another unsuccessful escape attempt. Frank you are forgetting we were caught red handed after killing those two fuckin Norfolk, Virginia cops. The local Carbone Mafia Cartel does not want any possible tie backs to that crime, whether we are family or not. Frank all I can tell you is that we are rated high on the GHVSP shit list as known "Cop Killers" so watch my back and I will watch yours. For now, just let's take our time, somehow, we will figure out what that Mafia note means and why it just speaks to "MGTH" and "SHE".

Doug, I do not know if you have noticed it or not, but inmates Don Lawson and Dick Horton across the corridor in holding cell No. 200 have not been seen for the last couple of days. Both of them were convicted of first degree murder in Richmond, Virginia. Rumors on the street say they can be found at the bottom of the "Big Lake". Frank who told you that shit? Old Henry Johnson when he delivered our food trays this morning. Old Henry Johnson told me he has been incarcerated in this Virginia State Prison system for thirty two years and that the "Big Lake" contains many mysteries many taking place long before this GHVSP was constructed here on this site.

Doug, I ask old Henry Johnson if he has ever seen the "Big Lake"? He told me yes, he has, that it is huge in size and well hidden deep within the main cavern of the "MGTH" in a separate seldom used branch of the mine. Old Henry Johnson said in order to find it you have to follow the mine rail car tracks from the branch switch off, all the way to the end where the mine car track block is located. Once there look at the "Big Lake" edge and locate a stone formation that spells out the word "SHE". SOB, Frank we may be on to something here. Did you ask old Henry Johnson what the stone formation and the word "SHE" means. Hell no, as he was in a hurry and running behind as one of the guards came quickly walking over to check on us and to get him ass moving. Doug if I get a chance, I will ask him tomorrow but I know he is being watched very closely and I know he does not want to take any chances and lose his cushy prison trustee position. Doug, we need to take it slow and not jeopardize him as he is fast becoming a close friend and a special inside point of contact (**POC**). Bill Nettles who works in the MGTH with us tells me old Henry Johnson can supply you with almost anything within reason from the outside world if the cash and the price is right.

Chapter 3

THE GHVSP SECRET MEETINGS

April 14, 1939. Friday morning about 0800Hr Chief Warden Kenneth Foster has called his two Assistant Wardens Lt Erma Kersay, Lt Jason Mitchell and his Security Force Captain Charles Stanton to his office for their usual private "Special Five" Quarterly Secret Meeting. He uses this meeting sometimes for General Purposes but for the most part they discuss illicit finances that satisfy their embezzlement gains and greed. (Remember Greed is the worse word in any language and is the root to all that is evil). With everyone as called in attendance and seated the Chiefs private secretary Peggy (Peg) Vinsen locks the door and closes all the interior shades and gets everyone a hot cup of coffee. Peg nods to the Chief that the office door is secured and goes and sits down at her desk. Sitting next to Peg is James Rawls Jr. (Jim). Jim is the GHVSP T/CPA. Jim is well educated; strait laced all business and answers only to the Chief and the Virginia State Treasurer Wesley Howard (Wes) a.k.a. in secret (The Big Man). Jim is meticulous in his work. He keeps two sets of Finance Books. One book is to cover the GHVSP records and expenses. This Finance book of course is reviewed every year by the Virginia State Treasures Auditors Office. The other Finance book is a well kept secret and known only to him and the Chief. A Penitentiary Mystic. This book contains all records and expenses related to the GHVSP Slush Fund and shows all the illicit gains collected and paid out in cash to the "Special Five" who are; Erma, Jason, Charles, Wesley and of course The Chief, Kenneth Foster. These books are kept under lock and key in Jim's office in separate locations never together of course.

The Chief opens the meeting with a happy announcement that the Honorable Governor of Virginia Christian Robb recently approved and signed a document that pays all State Prison Inmates one dollar a day for their labor related services. This of course brings forth a subdued quiet cheer from everyone as the GHVSP Slush Fund will skim off six dollars a month from each inmate as a self induced handling tax payment. As the Chief continues, he announces more good news as the sales of his cheap bootlegged whiskey a.k.a. "Syrup", tobacco and other miscellaneous concessions have also greatly increased. Great, more money for the GHVSP Slush Fund. (The Special Five are on a roll and doing very well).

Jim, do you have any special financial issues that you need to put on the table and discuss at this time. Yes, Chief starting this Quarter ending on march 31.1939 I will hand carry all GHVSP Slush Fund Allowances to you "Special Five" members in cash and in equal amounts. This will assure everyone they are receiving these payments on time. This will satisfy a complaint from the "Big Man" Peg brought to me that he has received his last two GHVSP Slush Fund payments late. I told Peg that if the "Big Man" calls with more complaints to just tell them to go get fucked that I am doing the best that I can. Chief that's all that I have at this time.

As this meeting continues the Chief brings up another issue that has the State's Governor's Office very concerned; and that is the sudden drop in sales of the GHVSP Mined Products to the Public. Charles, can you speak to this problem? Yes, Chief we just do not have any GHVSP (Interior or Exterior) mine products left over to sell to private contractors. Everything we produce from both mine's; granite blocks and crushed gravel is being consumed by the State for its own use. SOB Charles, the "Big Man" is not to going to be very happy to hear that shit. I realize that Chief but you cannot get blood out of a fuckin Turnip, shit happens. Maybe so Charles but I sure can get a piece of the turnip's ass.

Charles do we still have Old man Aubrey West and his Son's Mine Engineering Company (Co.) under contract? Yes sir, we certainly do, they Supervise all of our mine work above ground and below. Well, you tell Old man Aubrey West to get off his lazy fuckin ass we need GHVSP mine surplus products to sell to the Public. You tell, that old greedy bastard he has at his disposal all the GHVSP inmate labor he needs. Just use and put these worthless bastards to work!!!!!!! Yes Sir. I will speak with him later today right after this meeting is over. PLEASE DO!!!!!!!

Folks that's all that I have, is there any questions, if not this meeting is complete. Peg will schedule our next "Special Five" Quarterly meeting for some time in early July. If other items come up, I will call for a General Meeting to discuss those. Go, stay safe as we are all working in a very dangerous environment every day. Remember everything we discussed stays in this room loose tongues can cause a lot of waves. Remember my door is always open. Charles you and Jim stay a while longer I need to discuss this GHVSP mine product problem a little further with you off the cuff.

April 14, 1939. Friday it is now about 1030Hr. Everyone leaves the Chief's office except Charles, Jim and Peg. Peg again secures the door and nods to the Chief all clear. The Chief looks Charles directly in the face and states once again; Charles, get that fuckin Aubrey West and his son off their asses and work those worthless fuckin inmates we need more surplus GHVSP mine products to sell to the Public. If this does not take place soon the Governor is going to send some of his fuckin inspection hoods up here from Richmond snooping around and we must not let that take place. Those AH are nothing but fuckin trouble!

Chief I did not want to speak out in front of the others but we are producing and selling a reasonable amount of GHVSP mine products as we speak but most of the Public Sale moneys are being hidden in the GHVSP Slush Fund. All these sales are handled under cover for us by Aubrey West and his son. What the hell do you want me to do to offset this problem? Jim what is the market price across the board at this time for our mine products? One hundred dollars per ton for block stone and or crushed gravel. Is that a fair price? Yes sir, its well below market so we have no problem selling all the product we can produce plus it is in high demand. Well, let's do this; Charles instruct Aubrey West to start selling all of our surplus GHVSP Mine Products above board to all legit public customers for one hundred and fifty dollars a ton. Jim, cook all the paper work and the books to still just indicate the one hundred dollar a ton price. This will show the Governor and his hoods public sales have increased and this will get the AH off of our back. Skim off the other fifty dollars per ton and put it in the GHVSP Slush Fund. Charles just continue to settle up with Old man Aubrey

West and his son as usual. By the way Charles what does his pay off amount too? Chief he and his son each drive home a two and a half ton truck load of crushed gravel every evening after work. SOB Charles that fuckin greedy AH is making out like a bandit that amounts to $750 a day. I know, hell Chief do you want me to reduce his payoff. Hell let's not get greedy and piss him off. So what, who the hell is the crooked old bastard going to run too? Not only that one of my prison trustees that helps out in the GHQM told me Aubrey steals and takes a truck load of gravel home at lunch time every now and then. SOB Charles he is one crooked old bastard. Jim just shakes his head and thinks to himself; Ken Foster and Charles Foster two of the biggest crooks in the state of Virginia calling Old Aubrey West a crook, is that not the pot calling the kettle black! What a JOKE!

Charles while I have you and Jim here what is the latest on our GHVSP "Planned Vacation Program" a.k.a. "Planned Escapes". Chief things are slow to none at this time. Inmates Don Lawson and Dick Horton were the last two to leave us on Planned Vacations. Did they succeed? Yes sir, as far as we know! Jim handles the finances on those, I just set the escape plans up. Jim, can you update us did those two pieces of shit (POS) make it out of here safely? Evidently as I received the $50K gratuity from the local Carbone Mafia Cartel. I understand both Lawson and Horton were high level Caporegimes (Capos) in New York City and important enough that the Mafia Cartel paid our price to spring them. Charlie did you cover it well on our end? Yes sir, no problems what so ever.

Chief I set it up as I did years ago for William Lentz and Paul Daly. If you remember they were family members of Harrison Paul Daly the local Carbone Mafia Cartel "Don" (Boss). Both of them also worked out of New York City as Capos and Pro Hit men for the Carbone Mafia Cartel Murder Incorporated

Program. All four of these inmates have been reported to the Virginia State Attorney's Office as never seen again and presumed dead on the bottom of the "Big Lake" drowned while trying to escape. No questions asked, just another Penitentiary Mystic. Hell, Chief let's face it, trying to escape by swimming in cold deep water with a ball and chain attached to your fuckin ankle is nearly impossible, HA, HA! As they all laugh. Jim is the "Big Lake" the only safe Avenue of Escape from the GHVSP? Yes, Chief it's the only one I know about and it is only known to you, Charles, Peg and me. We only tell the escapee how to use this avenue when Charles sets up their escape plans.

Chief if you can swim and locate the escape tunnel you can disappear unseen using the "Old Wood Trail". The only other method requires the use of Lolly Dolly Road. As you know this road crosses through stripped opened land that offers no concealment. Using Lolly Dolly Road to try and escape at this time would be suicide. Jim, how were you able to figure out this "Big Lake" Avenue of escape, or did inmates find it accidently while searching The Big Lake Caverns for other rumored avenues as they do now? No Chief I figured it out on my own from childhood memories as a young boy years ago. Interesting!

Hell, Chief I looked at it this way; most of these inmates are serving life with no chance for parole and the easiest and safest way to escape from any prison in Virginia is to buy your way out. They all know this and it takes place all the time throughout the Virginia State Prison System. Money talks and BS walks! No tickee, No laundry! Important folks especially high level experienced Carbone Mafia Cartel folks are needed on the outside to expand necessary Mafia Cartel plans throughout the U.S.A. The Carbone Mafia Cartel has the money and they are willing pay the price to get these people back. So, I said shit, lets cash in. So having some friends in High and Low places we met together one night in secret and set up this Avenue of Escape. I ran it by Charles, he agreed and we put it in place, so far it seems to work to our advantage when we need it. SOB Jim will you and Charles run this amazing plan of yours by me step by step? All I have ever heard about it and any other GHVSP escape plans have been BS stories and BS rumors.

Chapter 4

AVENUE OF ESCAPE FROM THE GHVSP

April 14, 1939. Friday afternoon Charles, Jim and Peg continue to remain in the Chiefs office to satisfy his request to discuss the "Big Lake" Escape Plan from the GHVSP and how it was developed, set up and put in place. Like the Chief said all he has ever heard about the escape plan is based on rumors no true facts. He is now asking for complete details and facts.

Charles looks over at Jim and tells him to proceed as it is his plan and he handles all the details i.e. dates, pickups, gratuities and contracts. Well Chief do you really want me to spend the time and start from the very beginning? Yes, Jim I sure do! We all have light workloads this afternoon so I want you to take your time and give us all the details and steps involved. OK Chief but right up front I want to ask you please do not repeat any of this outlined story to anyone for any reason as Charles and I are the only ones knowledgeable of these specific details. If outsiders discover these specific detail's they could shut down our future escape plans and put us out of business. No worry, Jim I realize what is at stake here and where we all stand. Well, let me start all the way back to the day I was born. SOB, as they all laugh, HA! HA! Jim, I did not realize you were going back that fuckin far in time. Well, you AH you know me and you said you wanted to hear the entire story. Yes, I did! Jim, please continue you are telling this story I am sorry I interrupted you. Please Chief do not interrupt me again as I plan on telling this story in the first person as a small boy and as I remember it.

{Jim begins to tell his story; Well back on April 01,1904 when I was born my wonderful God Fearing father a well educated young Geological Mining Engineer accepted a job with the Dolly Family Mining Company located here in Virginia. At that time the Dolly Family owned and operated three different Granite Mines in different parts of the State. One, the Reddish Knob Mine near the Virginia, West Virginia State line within the Allegheny Mountains. Two, the Ramsey Draft Mine just outside of Deerfield in the Shenandoah Valley Blue Ridge. Three, this one the Green Heron Lake Mine here just outside of Carrisbrook.

My father with his experience and education was given a position at this Green Heron Lake Mine as Head Supervisor Controlling all Operations. Right away my father had problems dealing with Mr. Herman Dolly the wealthy Mine Company sole owner who wanted to micromanage his every move. As time passed dealing with Mr. Dolly became a major problem and my father told Mr. Dolly he could no longer be a "Yes Man" and submitted his resignation papers. Mr. Dolly not wanting to lose my father's experience relented, finally got the message and stepped aside.

As time continued to pass the mine operated very well and product production was set at a reasonable level that included both the exterior strip mine operation and the interior "Big Lake" cavern mine operation. No problems except Mr. Dolly begin to get greedy. (Remember "Greed" is the worse word in any language, it is the root to all that is evil). Mr. Dolly decided he wanted all of his miners to work harder and increase production as the demand for his granite products was high and the market price was at a record high level.

Never satisfied Mr. Dolly told my father he wanted more miners on the job, working harder and longer hours. To make matters worse he set his miners pay rate at a low standard and introduced the "Dolly Mining Co. Token Program". Take it or leave it. This token program paid the miners 50% in wages and 50% in Dolly Co. tokens. The straw that broke the camel's back was that these Co. tokens could only be used at The Dolly Mining Co. Stores to purchase overpriced food and medical supplies. With no other jobs available and unemployment high in the area the miners had no choice but to accept Mr. Dolly's demands.

All of this greed and these demands became too much for my father to except and deep inside he became very enraged and decided to present a long time thought out plan to the miners. On one very rare day when Mr. Dolly reported in sick; my father saw his chance and summoned all the miners here together in a secret meeting held at the entrance of the interior "Big Lake" mine. There he instructed and help the miners to set up a "Mine Workers Union". This of course begin a movement that affected mine operations at all three Dolly Co. Mine locations. A movement that Mr. Dolly could not and would not tolerate.

Not knowing my father was the Secret Organizer of this Union movement Mr. Dolly ordered him to clamp down and put a stop to this so called Union nonsense. My father told Mr.

Dolly he would do what he could but the Mine Workers Union was too far advanced and that a Miners Strike was scheduled to take place at all three of the Dolly Mines in the very near future. Hearing this very disturbing news involving a miners strike Mr. Dolly increased his security force and hired a bunch of street thugs. Things got worse and Mr. Dolly ordered these street thugs to weed out and eliminate in any way possible the Union Leaders and any other Trouble Makers. As these orders were carried out people begin to disappear at all three Dolly Mine locations. All of a sudden here at the Green Heron Lake Mine location Union Leaders Richard Bains and Perry Norris disappeared. Where are they, where did they go? To this day no one really knows. Well sad to say these disappearances did the job and the miners afraid of losing their jobs and or mysteriously disappearing relented and stopped their movement plans.

On June 06, 1914. Saturday evening about 1800Hr my father and I rode over to the Green Heron Lake Mine. As we slowly approached the interior Mine entrance, we noticed two men getting in to one of the mine rail cars and driving down inside the mine. My father quickly parked and staying quiet and hopefully unseen we followed the mine rail car on foot. It seemed like we walked for miles and believe me I was really getting tired out.

Finally, we arrived deep inside this huge cavern beside this enormous underground lake, the "Big Lake". To me this lake was beautiful enormous in size and it seemed to go on forever. The mine rail car we followed was stopped at a dead end track block. The two men got out of the mine rail car and lifted two steel drums out of a rack on the mine rail car. They rolled and loaded the drums on to an outboard motor boat. One man stayed back on shore while the other one drove the boat well off shore almost out of sight. A few minutes later he drove the boat back to the pier and tied it up. As they both got back in the mine rail car, we heard him tell his buddy he dumped both drums in the usual deep water area like before, they will never be found that's for damn sure. All I can say is TYDL for keeping those overhead mine lights on.

June 06, 1946. Saturday about 2000Hr my father and I with great caution followed the mine rail car slowly back to the mines main entrance. Well hidden behind a stack of granite blocks we watched as the two men my father could now clearly see and recognize as Steve Moor and Curtis Clark two new Dolly Co. Security Force street thugs get in a Dolly Co. truck and leave. My father and I watched until the truck was well out of sight before we walked over and got in to his Dolly Co. truck and drove home. When we returned back home, I could see from the sad expression on my father's face he was very upset. My mother of course recognized this and had him sit down and relax while she got him a glass of merlot wine. As they both sat at the kitchen table discussing what he and I just witnessed and the possible crime involved, the conversation begin to take on serious tones. That's when they decided I had heard enough and should just get cleaned up and go to bed. I did what they told me but to upset and to excited to sleep I quietly sat on the hallway floor behind the archway opening curtain and continued to listen to my parents talk.

As my father now a little settled down sipped on his wine, my mother asks him what he planned to do! Linda Mae, I am not sure! I need to notify the authorities as I am sure Jimmy and I may have witnessed the disposal of the two local Union Leaders Richard Baines and Perry Norris being dumped in to the "Big Lake". Linda Mae if this is the case Steve Moor and Curtis Clark are two cold blooded murders working under strict orders from Herman Dolly. If those two ever found out Jimmy and I witnessed this possible crime they would track us down and kill us both. Linda Mae what do you think I should do at this time?

Well Jim one of the first things we need to do is fully discuss this with Jimmy in the morning and make him realize he must never speak of this possible crime to anyone ever. As for now I would telephone the nearest VSBI Field Office and report this possible crime to them, give them all the details as you remember them and let them take over. Jim for God's sake do not tell them who you are other than a Dolly Mine employee working late and overtime. To be on the safe side make your call from the outside telephone booth up at "Phills Filling Station, Pub and Auto Repair up on the street corner. Phills stays open all night on Saturdays. Go now and drive the car and not your Dolly Co. truck. Let's see its 2230Hr go now I will stay here with Jimmy you might as well get it over with. Linda Mae you are right as usual let me get going.

June 07, 1914. Sunday morning about 0100Hr my dad is back home safely. Mom of course hears him drive up and runs to the back door to let him in. Mom asks him my Lord Jim what kept you so long you had me worried to death. Well Linda Mae the telephone operator put my call straight through to the Richmond VSBI Field Office collect no problems but the connection service out here is terrible as it comes and goes. I did luck out as the line was direct and not on a party line system. TYDL.

Anyway, the VSBI Agent on duty wrote down all the details I was able to give him letter by letter. When I mentioned Mr. Herman Dolly may be involved, he stuttered and quietly said "Holy Shit"!!!!!! He said sir I do not know who you are but Mr. Dolly is one of the most powerful men in this state; hell, he has most of the crookest politicians local and state in his hip pocket and some even on his pay roll? I told him I did not care that

Mr. Dolly hired those two thugs and if a crime was committed, he was as guilty as they are. About that time the telephone line went dead. The telephone Operator tried several times to call back. All she could tell me is that all the lines were dead. I gave up and as I was walking to the car to come home a Dolly Mine Co. truck pull in and parked beside me. Would you believe inside the truck was Steve Moor and Curtis Clark? They saw me hollered and insisted I come in to Phills Pub and drink a beer. Both of them were very drunk but to pacify them I told them hell yes why not let's go! I drank one beer slapped them both on the back laughed and said I will see you two guys Monday morning on the job. They both laughed said OK old buddy and I left. Linda Mae just being around those two thugs and possible murders makes me feel dirty. I know hon! Do not worry things will work out, like my mom always said "it comes home"!

June 07, 1914. Sunday morning about 1130Hr Mom, Dad and I pull in to the driveway just getting back home from church. I jumped out of the car and started to run quickly into the house. Father hollered hold up Jimmy what's your hurry? I told him I was going to skip lunch as I was in a hurry to get over to Butlers Lake to meet my two friends Sammy T. Jones and Billy H. Thomas. No way you need to stay and eat lunch first as your mother and I need to talk with you, just go on in the house change your clothes and go be seated at the kitchen table, NOW! Being very upset I did what I was told to do. At the kitchen table mom and dad explained to me what I already knew was coming and expected. They did make me realize how important it was not to ever speak to anyone about the possible murder crime dad and I witnessed last Saturday evening especially to my two buddies Sammy and Billy. I told them no worry I got the message loud and clear. To this day I have kept my word and have not ever told a soul until now.

Finally, I got permission to leave and as I was walking out the door my father asks me what are you three guys going to do all day. I told him swim in Butlers Lake over off Woods Trail. All he just said was be careful have a good time and be very careful and for God's Sake do not trespass on the adjacent nearby Dolly Green Heron Lake Mining Co. property. Finally, for what seemed like a life time I got over to Butlers Lake. I met up with Sammy and Billy and as usual we all went skinny dipping. The water was warm, clear and beautiful and we were all having a ball. As I was swimming in this very clear water, I noticed what appeared as a light just below the surface on the edge of the lake. Being very curious and a stupid ten year old kid I dived down and discovered this very small tunnel. All excited I went top side and told Billy and Sammy what I had discovered. I told them what the hell lets go and check it out. We all agreed took a deep breath and down we went. We dived down about four feet and swam through this very small lighted tunnel a few yards and surfaced inside this massive cavern in this huge lake. As we all just marveled at our discovery, I suddenly realized I was in the "Big Lake" inside the cavern were my father and I had been Saturday. As I looked around, I saw the mine rail car track block and the motor boat tied to the Dolly Mining Co. pier. Knowing I could not say anything to my buddies about being here before I just let it go and acted just as surprised and excited as they were. One thing for sure we knew we had discovered a Paradise. A Big Lake to swim in, a motor boat to run and fish in and best of all electric mine rail cars to ride in.

As we came ashore to do more exploring, we noticed a big steel pad locked Red Painted Door. This door was labeled "Authorized Personnel Only" "Explosive Devices". Having seen enough for now we decided to swim back to Butlers Lake rest lie on the beach and chat about our new found Playground

Paradise. All of a sudden, we found ourselves lost, the location of the tunnel was not visible on the "Big Lake" side. Holy Shit, after a few frantic dives we located the small tunnel opening and swam back through to Butler's Lake. Finally relieved, safe and sound lying on the beach we realized the sunlight help locate the tunnel from the Butler Lake side but on the "Big Lake" side the mine lights and the dark cavern interior was not enough to outline the tunnel opening. To locate it we had to mark it in some way. So, what the hell do three ten year old geniuses do? Would you believe Billy comes up with an idea so stupid we liked it? Look here as he reaches in his knap sack and pulls out this Pamphlet. Look here let's use this. The word "SHE" it means "Satan & Hells Exit", read all about it. Billy where did you get this? Some religious group was handing them out yesterday downtown. I looked at Sammy he said what the hell let's go and do it. All three of us swam back and marked the beach above the tunnel opening with the word "SHE" spelling it out using small pieces of granite stone set in place. Folks that's my story. "FINNEE"}. End of Jim's Story.

April 14, 1939. Friday afternoon about 1230Hr. Well Chief that's my story as well as I can remember it as described in the first person by a ten year old boy, any questions? Jim let me get this straight; are you telling me an escapee has to find his way through the GHQM to the "Big Lake", locate (using the word "SHE") and swim down through a hidden tunnel, come up on the outside somewhere in "Butlers Lake" soaking wet and walk about two miles down through the "Old Wood Trail" to Rt 250 and meet an arranged pickup by a Carbone Mafia Cartel Capo to complete his paid for "Planned Vacation"? YES SIR, I CERTAINLY AM!!!! Chief that's my story and I am sticking to it, like it or not!!!!!! Charles, can you add anything? No sir, Jim has it absolutely correct "Swim or Drown". No tickee, No laundry! Chief when I set the escape up, the escapee knows what to expect. It's not my job to forgive and help him that is decided in a meeting between him and the Good Lord, my job is to set up this meeting, done deal! Any more questions Chief? No, not at this time it looks like you and Jim have all the bases covered. The Chief shakes his head and says; unreal!

Chapter 5

HOW ARE THE PLANNED VACATIONS PAID FOR

April 14, 1939. Friday about 1330Hr Jim and Peggy leave the Chiefs office and drive down Lolly Dolly Road on the way to lunch. Hell Peg, where would you like to go and eat lunch. Hell Jim let's just go to our usual booth at Phills Pub, one of his big chili dogs loaded with onions and a cold draft beer would hit the spot. Sounds good to me. As they sit and chat at Phills Pub Peg asks Jim why he cut some corners when telling them all about the Escape Plans, you never said a word about the "Big Lake" or about the "Red Door". Well, I am working on several plans involving them if possible as a backup. I will tell you about those plans later if I decide to put them in place. Oh shit, not more Penitentiary Mystics.

Jim, do you think the Chief knows anything about our relationship? I doubt it he is too busy counting his GHVSP Slush Fund money and kissing his own greedy ass. What about

Charles? Peg Charles does a lot of snooping around so you do need to keep your eyes on him. Hell, I walked in to his office last Thursday and the AH had Erma bent over his desk with her skirt up over her head banging away. Hell, I just backed off said I am sorry Charles I will come back later when you are not so tied up having pie at the "Y" and getting your joint greased. I laughed, closed the door and left. Damn Peg you should have seen them scramble and the expressions on their faces, they just about shit. Charles came by my office later and ask me to keep what I saw on the Qts. I told him no worry and tell Erma I did not see a thing that fuckin on your spare time is fun and none of my business. He just grinned walked out and said he owed me one.

Jim, do you plan on telling the Chief about what you, Sam and Bill later discovered while swimming in the "Big Lake"? No Peg let's keep that our secret for now, they will find out sooner or later I will make sure of that. Jim how many steel drums did you three boys find over the years in the "Big Lake"? OH Lord Peg dozens or more but God only knows how many are out in the really deep water you will never find or ever know about, that damn lake has no bottom.

Jim, do you suppose all of those steel drums contain persons murdered by street thugs hired by Old Man Herman Dolly? Peg I am not sure of that, we will probably never know but I would think that's the case because all of our discoveries occurred when we were young boys long before the Dolly Family sold this huge mine complex to the State of Virginia. Peg however do not forget this, since those early years and since the GHVSP opened, many Penitentiary Inmate escapees and trouble makers have been lost to mine accidents or presumed drown never to be seen again. Some of these of course you and I know about have been Carbone Mafia Cartel Buy Outs under our "Planned Vacation Program".

Jim, you always tell me about the "Red Door" but you have never told me how you got in or what you three boys actually found other than a few more empty steel drums. Well on one of our outings we decided to go swimming in the "Big Lake" and ride the mine rail cars. Knowing where the mine rail car keys are located, I opened the electrical panel box to get the keys and this other key fell out that was labeled "Red Door Storage". I said hell guys lets go check it out. Hell Peg, no problem the key easily unlocked the door and we all walk in like we owned the place. The lights were already on. As we snooped around, we saw the usual tools related to Granite Mining work and Mine Rail Car Repairs. In one area we saw several large heavy wooden boxes of Nitroglycerin Charged Dynamite, Pure Trinitrotoluene (TNT) and some labeled, explosion caps, wires and ignition caps.

As we continued snooping, we found about twenty empty steel drums. Getting bored looking at this junk we decided to leave and go ride some Mine Rail Cars when Sammy pulled a tarp off of some separate covered steel drums in another isolated area. All those drums were tightly closed except one that had a popped loose lid. Sammy looked inside screamed and fell backwards. Hell, he hollered and said guys you better come over here and look at this. We all looked in disbelief; the drum was filled with crushed gravel covering a human body with one hand slightly exposed.

Peg to be three young tough guys that wrote the book we all got sick on our stomachs. Sammy looked at me and Billy and said do you suppose all these drums contain human bodies. Probably so let's just get the fuck out of here and go home it's something about this place that's getting very strange and creepy.

Damn Jim, I cannot believe you three guys did not report this terrible discovery to the local authorities. Peg, I cannot tell you why. Something just told us to go home and forever remain silent. Hell Peg, it's another "Big Lake" Cavern Mystic.

April 14, 1939. Friday afternoon about 1430Hr back at the GHVSP Jim walks Peg back up to her and the Chiefs office as he wants to ask the Chief a question involved with some invoices. As they walk in Jim sees Charles and the Chief having a heated discussion involved with the GHVSP Slush Fund. Jim, just the man we want to see will you please briefly tell us how the Planned Vacations are Paid for and how you handle these Carbone Mafia Cartel Gratuities? Charles and I have a slight disagreement on how this is taken care of. No problem, Chief its very simple and fool proof. When I receive notification regrading a certain GHVSP inmate the Carbone Mafia Cartel would like released in my pick up box they state the Gratuity Amount they are willing to pay, usually $50K per person which in most cases is acceptable by me. This pick up box is a small Blue Bird House I have installed on a tree along the Old Wood Trail entrance out near Rt 250. If you notice when you drive by, there is a turn around and small parking area created by the kids that they use when they park to go skinny dipping in Butlers Lake.

I check this Blue Bird House pick up box several times a week. My POC or friends in low or high places are known only to me. I always receive this information in brief notes from them never any telephone calls or anything traceable back to my GHVSP office or my home. Anyway, after I receive this note, I in turn pass the inmates name on to Charles. He in turn sets up the Escape Plan following our standard procedures we have already discussed. In detail they are: Step 1. The inmate is assigned to a GHQM work detail. Step 2. There he is instructed to drive a mine rail car to the seldom used "Big Lake" area all the way to the mine rail car track block. Step 3, Once there, look along the lake shore line and locate the word "SHE" spelled out in stones. Walk over to those stones and dive down about four feet find and swim through a very small tunnel to "Butlers Lake". Step 4. Walk soaking wet along the "Old Wood Trail" to Rt 250. There you will find a Carbone Mafia Cartel car driven by a Capo that will give you a towel, new dry clothes and drive you safely to Norfolk, Virginia. Note: Be sure to use the hacksaw found in the mine rail car tool box to remove your ball and chain anklet. Chief at this time after the inmate pickup is secured the same Mafia Capo will place the agreed to Gratuity in cash in the Blue Bird House pick up box. I pick it up later and add it to the GHVSP Slush Fund safe deposit box. Done deal any questions! None what so ever it appears you and Charles have all the bases covered.

Jim, are there any planned Vacations (Escapes) at this time? No not at this time things are slow, far and few. The last two inmates seeking Planned Vacations were Don Lawson and Dick Horton two well known and experienced Carbone Mafia Cartel Capos from New York City. That deal is closed and settled. Chief at this time I do have a problem that has me puzzled. We have two inmates Doug Lentz and Frank Daly that are well known family members of the local Hampton Roads Carbone Mafia Cartel "Don", Harrison Paul Daly; Frank is his youngest son and Doug is his nephew. Under normal conditions they should have been sprung months ago, I wonder what the holdup is? Good question Jim, check with prison trustee old Henry Johnson if anyone knows what is going on it will be him.

Well fellows I am well up to date thanks to you two guys (Jim & Charles). But Jim I do have one question? Fire away Chief. Years ago, when your father telephoned the VSBI to report the possible crime you two witnessed was there any follow up? Was Herman Dolly and his two street thugs Steve Moor and Curtis Clark ever investigated or arrested? Yes, but only to the degree the VSBI wanted to show it was on going. My father told my mother later that it was all covered up in BS. It went in the official VSBI records to indicate a crime was not seen or committed. Hell, Chief those VSBI Agents that investigate that possible crime never questioned any Dolly Mining Co. staff members. Hell Jim, it just goes to show you when you have friends in high and low places money talks and BS walks. Chief you got that right, tell me about it! Jim its none of my business but is your father still employed by the Dolly Family Mining Co. Lord no! He resigned years ago and took a job with the Zion Cross Roads Mining Co. He is about sixty years old and planning on retiring soon. He told me last weekend he is tired and just wants to get out from under it all.

Chapter 6

WILL DOUG LENTZ AND FRANK DALY SING

April 14,1939. Friday afternoon about 1630Hr Charles and Jim leave the Chiefs office to continue their official GHVSP duties. Peg stays at her desk and the Chief at his. As Jim leaves, he gives Peg a big simile and displays a small victory sign with one hand meaning its "Pie at the "Y" time. Peg knowing what it means nods and grins back. The Chief as usual is caught up in his greedy thoughts as he thinks about his slice of the GHVSP Slush Fund monies. Like everyone else his age he is ready to retire and move to his little cottage on the Piankatank River, drink beer, fish and fuck. Peg straightens up her desk and asks the Chief if he needs anything, before she leaves for the day? Yes, Peg on your way out drop this letter in the U. S. mail box down stairs. Have a good evening and I will see you bright and early tomorrow morning. As Peg drops the letter in the mail box, she notices it is addressed to the Virginia State Treasurer

Wes Howard, she also knows Wes is one of the "Special Five" a.k.a. "The Big Man".

As Peg leaves the GHVSP she drives down Lolly Dolly Road stops and turns East on to Rt 250. As she drives down Rt 250 she glances over and sees the turn around Jim spoke about in his story and decides to pull over and stop. Curious she gets out and looks around, seeing the coast is clear she decides to walk a short distance down the "Old Wood Trail" and find Jim's pickup box, the Blue Bird House. After walking a few yards, she spots the Blue Bird House and just for the hell of it removes the top and glances inside and removes an unsealed envelope and reads the enclosed note. The note reads; Inmates Doug Lentz and Frank Daly must be eliminated ASAP as ordered by the Carbone Family Mafia Cartel. They both know too much about the new planned Biloxi Mississippi Mafia Cartel Operations. GHVSP inside rumors indicate they have plans in place with the FBI and the VSBI to expose this information in exchange for a deal involving the Federal Witness Protection Program. Set up Planned Vacations for these two inmates ASAP but when doing so instead of releasing them eliminate them and make it appear as an accident. A substantial Gratuity of $200K for each will be awarded when this contract is confirmed and complete.

Peg is totally stunned and cannot believe anyone would send out orders directing the Murder of their own son or other family members. But she also realizes the Carbone Mafia Family Cartel does not take prisoners for any reason. Peg carefully puts the note back in the Blue Bird House as she found it. She feels ashamed as she knows the note contains secret information she may not have been allowed to hear, read or see. Not only that she betrayed a trust between her and Jim and knows he would be very upset should he find out she had found this note and read it behind his back.

Peg feeling very guilty gets in her car and slowly drives home. Back home she takes a shower dresses sexy and starts to fix supper as Jim pulls in the driveway. Jim walks in, still feeling very guilty about her snooping she gives him a big kiss and says steaks are on the grill, merlot wine and sharp cheese is poured, cut and sitting on the table and "Pie at the "Y" for desert will be served later. SOB, I need to start working more overtime. Sweetheart you are really spoiling me tonight please do not stop I love every minute. As they both settle down and sip on a glass of merlot wine Jim tells her he stopped by his Blue Bird House pick up box on the way home and picked up this very disturbing note from the local Mafia Cartel as he hands it to her to read. Peg takes the note and feeling a sense of relief from her guilt and snooping reads it and pretends she is shocked and never has seen it before. She also realizes Jim fully trusts her and she will never go behind his back again for any reason.

After reading the note she asks Jim what are you going to do? Peg, I have no choice I am caught up in a catch 22. I am a major player in the illegal GHVSP Planned Vacation (Escape) Program with the Chief, Charles and the Carbone Mafia Cartel. I will follow the usual procedures and past this information on to the Chief and Charles Monday morning and let the chips fly where they may. Charles can set it up and have them both (Lentz and Daly) eliminated while trying to escape. Peg, I know it's a sad situation to be in but once onboard with the Carbone Mafia Cartel you follow the rules or take a one way drum ride on a boat out on the Chesapeake Bay. Do not worry my dear everything involving my secret plans and future for us is falling in place. After a few more details are settled I intend to go over these plans with you very soon. Jim I certainly hope so working at that Carbone Mafia Cartel Controlled GHVSP is beginning to wear me down. Well, my dear let's just eat those nice grilled steaks, that nice salad, sip some more merlot wine and relax. Hon, I do not know about you but my little bad boy is beginning to twitch and that tells me it's getting close to Pie time at the "Y", HA, HA! Peg just laughs and says, Jim you big AH you stay horny. He looks at her similes and replies, yes I do Peg, but you little bitch you love it.

April 17,1939. Monday morning about 0700Hr Jim and Peg drive separate cars to work so as not to make it so obvious they are a serious item. They walk into the GHVSP Administration Building. Jim tells her he will see her later for lunch as she catches the elevator up to her and the Chiefs office on the third floor. As usual the Chief is not in yet. She turns on the lights and puts on the coffee. As she sits quietly and sips on a cup of coffee, she plans her day as she scans her daily log. She realizes after what took place Friday that Jim will call and request a meeting with the Chief and Charles to discuss the Carbone Mafia Cartel note he received. About 0800Hr the Chief comes walking in. He smiles, says good morning to Peg and sits down at his desk as she gets him a cup of coffee. He sips on his coffee and asks Peg what is on the agender today? Well Chief, things are running so smoothly nothing but your usual general inspections and kick ass rounds. He laughs and tells her that's the way it's supposed to be when you run a tight fisted ship like I do. Peg just thinks to herself there he goes again kissing his own greedy ass and taking all the credit, boy is he a first class AH.

About that time the telephone rings. She picks it up and as expected its Jim. Peg, I have Charles in my office we would like to come up and discuss a problem that has just come up with the Chief. She looks over tells the Chief its Jim he and Charles need to come up and discuss a problem with you. Peg, tell them I am very busy at the moment but I can work them in about

1000Hr. Jim the Chief is busy at the moment but can work you in about 1000Hr. OK Peg, we will see you then.

April 17,1939. Monday morning about 1000Hr Jim and Charles come walking in to the Chiefs always open office door. They walk in and sit down as Peg gets them all a cup of coffee. Well guys what's on your mind what's this important problem you need to discuss with me? Chief it involves another "Planned Vacation" (Escape). What's so important about that, you and Charles handle it just like you have handled all the others. Well Chief it's not going to be that simple. Chief the Carbone Mafia Cartel want Inmates Douglas Lentz and Frank Daly to escape ASAP but they want them eliminated while doing so. Are you sure? Yes sir, not only that they want the elimination process to appear as an accident. Well, just have them listed as drowning victims in the "Big Lake", no problem, Charles just get it done. Chief it's not going to be that easy. Jim received this note last Friday requesting the elimination of these two inmates ASAP and they are willing to pay us $200K per man when its final. SOB Charles that's great that will really sweeten our GHVSP Slush Fund, more money for the "Special Five". Chief let me finish like I said it's not going to be that easy. Jim just received this follow up note this morning and the local Carbone Mafia Cartel, "Don" Harrison Paul Daly now wants the bodies of Lentz and Daly after they have been eliminated transported to the local "Pollock Funeral Home and Crematory" over in Carrisbrook for some unknown reason. There after positive identification and viewing by family members they will be cremated and their cremains picked up later. When that takes place the $400K Gratuity will be delivered to us at that same time.

Well Charles you and Jim set it up and let me see your final plans. Chief I am out of this, like I told you earlier I handle and pass along the requests and take care of the gratuities.

Charles sets up the Escape Plans and goes over the plans with the inmates involved. Well, GHVSP Security Force Captain Charles Stanton what the fuck do you suggest we do???? Chief I am not sure all I can think of at this time is have Lentz and Daly shot and killed by one of my GHVSP Security Force Guards while trying to escape in some way. Charles escaping "some way" what the hell does that BS "some way" mean? Put your fuckin "some way" plans on the fuckin table we are talking big bucks here, $400K is not chicken feed.

April 17, 1939. Monday morning it is now about 1130Hr Peg hears a knock on the Chiefs office door. Peg right away gets up and unlocks the door and steps outside. SOB Erma, when did you start delivering the mail? I don't but this is a special delivery letter that just came for the Chief that is marked urgent and I was in the mail room at the time so I offered to drop it by. Here Peg you need to sign off this receipt right here as authorized! OK, thank you Erma! As Erma walks off Peg laughs and whispers are you getting any hay for your donkey, I understand Charles has a desk full? Erma just gives Peg the finger and says fuck you everybody knows you are shacking up with Jim and fuckin his eyeballs out. Peg takes the letter back inside slams the door and locks it. Back at her desk she can see and hear the conversation between the Chief and Charles is becoming a little heated as Jim steps in and try's to settle them both down. Finally, the Chief just looks at Charles and says we cannot settle this now just cool down, go back to your office and work on a possible solution that will work an appear legit and look like an accident. OK Chief good idea it's not like it has to take place today.

As Charles and Jim stand up to leave Peg interrupts them and hands the Chief the special delivery letter she just finished reading. She knows all three men; the Chief, Charles and Jim are going to go ape shit when the Chief reads the letter to them. As the Chief quickly scans the letter he shouts "Holy Fuckin Shit". Charles says holy shit Chief what does the fuckin letter say? He quickly tells them the VSBI is sending Agents up here to remove GHVSP inmates Douglas Lentz and Frank Daly from the GHVSP. Please prepare them for planned releases and transfers on Friday April 28,1939 at 1400 Hr. These two inmates will now be held in Confinement at the Richmond, Virginia State Penitentiary at 500 Spring Street until a possible release under the Federal Witness Protection Program based on Secret Testimonies to the FBI and the VSBI is confirmed and verified. These are secret testimonies that will speak to Carbone Mafia Family Cartel Activities throughout the U.S.A. Please do not discuss the information or this letter with anyone. GHVSP Warden Kenneth Foster have your GHVSP Security Force Captain Charles Stanton place these two Inmates under a special security watch 24/7 for their own safety until this April 28, 1939 transfer takes place. Signed: Chief VSBI Agent Sean Nuttycombe. Richmond, Virginia Field Office.

The Chief throws the letter down on his desk and looks directly at Charles and says, make something happen and make it happen very fuckin fast, April 28,1939 is Friday week and these two fuckin bastards Doug Lentz and Frank Daly are going to start singing like a flock of new hatched yellow Canary birds and they have nothing to lose. Charles like I said put your "Some Way" plans on the table very damn quick. I do not want a bunch of Federal and State Law Enforcement people of any kind in my fuckin GHVSP snooping around for any reason.

Chapter 7

SIMPLE ESCAPE PLANS

April 17, 1939. Monday morning late about 1130Hr Jim and Charles leave the Chiefs office; as they walk down the long hallway Jim asks Charles what are you going to set up do you have any ideas in mind? Jim I am not sure do you have anything in mind? Charles you only have two choices. One is use, the GHQM, or two, use Lolly Dolly Road. Either way you eliminate them it has to appear as an accident and you need to keep the two bodies so they are viewable. Charles you can have security guards on duty and let them do the dirty work or you can do it yourself. Charles I would use Lolly Dolly Road. Let Lentz And Daly steal one of Aubrey West's Co. trucks and drive off in the sunset. Somewhere along the way have your security guards set up a planned roadblock, stop them and shoot the fuckin truck out from under them, done deal. That way you get to keep the two bodies for the Daly family to view at Pollocks Funeral Home in Carrisbrook and they can come back later and pick up the cremains as planned. Also keep in mind by doing this we do not risk the chance that an investigation will expose in anyway our "Big Lake", "SHE" escape route. Charles we cannot let that happen.

Jim, I like your Lolly Dolly Road idea. Let me think about that and work up a plan using that idea. OK Charles let me know if I can help you further in anyway. Great Jim let me run I need to go by and talk to Aubrey West and chew his ass out about producing more GHQM Products. As you know the "Big Man" wants more products produced for Public Sales. The greedy bastard is like the Chief the more they have the more they want. Like, I said Charles; "Greed is the root to all that is Evil".

April 17,1939. Monday about 1230Hr Jim calls Peg. Hi Jim I have been waiting for your call to take a lunch break, where too? Let's just run over to Phills Pub to our usual booth, its close by and the food is great. Hon meet me out front I will drive as I want to check out a few things along the way as we drive.

As Jim and Peg pass through the big front entrance gate of the GHVSP Jim begins to tell her about the Lolly Dolly Road Escape Plan Charles is setting up for inmates Doug Lentz and Frank Daly. Peg think about what I am telling you about his plan and please add your ideas. I told Charles I did not want to use our "Big Lake" set up and take a chance and have it exposed in any way. As they sit an chat in Phills Pub while eating lunch Jim asks Peg what she thinks about their Lolly Dolly Road Escape Plan? Jim, I guess it's as good as any, remember you are just going to murder these two poor bastards anyway just make it sound and look good to the VSBI Agents when they investigate. You know Chief VSBI Agent Sean Nuttycombe when he finds out these two have been killed is going to go ape shit as he has big plans involving their expected testimonies. You can bet your sweet ass he will have VSBI Agents swarming all over the GHVSP investigating how and why did this happen, especially at this time. Jim he is no dumb ass by any means!

Jim, just think about this: why would two inmates serving life long prison sentences ever try and take a chance to escape when they may have freedom handed to them on a silver platter for testimonies that expose a worthless Mafia Cartel Organization that would not offer them the usual buy outs? Hell Jim, if I was in their place, I would just stay safe in that holding cell until April 28, 1939 at 1400Hr and take my chances with the FBI and the VSBI. Peg what if the VSBI is setting them up, gets their testimonies, renege on the deal and just keeps them in the Virginia State Prison system for the rest of their lives? Jim, you know that will never happen. The VSBI cannot afford to renege on any Witness Protection Program or any other Program. If they did no one would ever come forward and support any criminal investigation for them again. If the Carbone Mafia Cartel wants these two inmates eliminated let them come forward and do the dirty work themselves not you and Charles. Peg I fully understand what you are saying but the Carbone Mafia Cartel has us all under their control. Believe it or not they control this entire GHVSP Complex lock stock and barrel. I have no choice and no way out at this time. Peg my future plans for us are falling in place, if they hold true, I can get you and me out from under this GHVSP Mafia mess. Like I said I will discuss these plans with you when I feel like they are safe and complete.

April 19, 1939. Wednesday morning about 0800Hr Charles calls Jim in his office. Hello! Jim it's me I have an escape plan in place I would like to discuss and run by you when would be a good time? Charles I am free now come on over now. About 0900Hr Charles walks in to Jim's office! Charles shuts the door tightly and locks it behind him and sits down. Jim gets them both a cup of hot coffee sits down and says lay it on the table Charles let's see what you have planned and it better be damn good. Peg said the Chief is going ape shit waiting to hear from you.

Well Jim it's a very simple plan. I will set up inmates Lentz and Daly to escape on their own on Monday morning April 24, 1939. This will give me time hopefully to convenience them that any Witness Protection Program the VSBI can offer them will never protect or hide them from the Carbone Mafia Cartel. That these Carbone Mafia Cartel people will eventually track them down and take them for a steel drum ride on a nice boat and dump them overboard in the Chesapeake Bay. Prison trustee old Henry Johnson said he will work with me on this as he is a close friend to both Doug and Frank.

Anyway, once I feel safe and sure they are convinced; on the morning of April 24, I will have them while on their GHQM work detail duties unload supplies from one of the Aubrey West Co. pickup trucks. While doing this they will find "West and Co. Coveralls in the truck along with Company hard hats they can put on as disguises. After they unload this fully fueled up truck they simply get in and drive off out and around the GHVSP outside wall and slowly down Lolly Dolly Road. As they approach the intersection of Lolly Dolly Road and Rt 250 they will be stopped by two guards on my security force; guards Patrick Payne and Russell Rice. They will know upfront this will be a routine stop and not a confrontation of any kind and not to be alarmed for any reason. After being stopped by my two guards they will each be handed a small box and told to open this box on their drive East on Rt 250 towards Richmond. A note in the box will tell them where to drive to and safely get picked up and leave the truck to be found. As they take these boxes my two guards simply shoot each man at point blank range in the head and a couple of times elsewhere making it look like an escape confrontation took place. Done Deal!

Well Jim what do you think? We have Doug Lentz and Frank Daly dead to rights while trying to escape, Aubrey West has his Company truck back undamaged, we notify Pollocks Funeral Home in Carrisbrook to come and remove the two dead bodies as already set in place by the local Carbone Mafia Cartel. You later drive by and pick up the $400K Gratuity at the Funeral Home as discussed and safely deposit it in our GHVSP Slush Fund and everyone goes dancing down the Fuckin "Yellow Brick Road" fat and sassy.

Charles, I like your plans but do you think it is well enough designed to convince the Chief VSBI Agent Sean Nuttycombe. Yes, because my two guards will place at the escape site two cheap revolvers normally used as throw aways by Mafia Hit men that were smuggled in with the usual inside and outside prison help. These two guards have been instructed to fire these two revolvers to spend a few rounds making it look like a shoot out took place doing a standard escape confrontation by two desperate escapees. Charles, I have another question? Go ahead! Why were your two guards posted at this Rt 250 intersection at this most convenient time to start with, hell that's not normal. Well Jim this is why I selected Monday April 24 to start with. My two guards Patrick Payne and Russell Rice were returning from Phills Filling Station and Pub on their routine GHVSP Vehicle Maintenance Plan Schedule. The State has a fixed contract in place with Phills Auto Repair to maintain the State GHVSP Vehicles, this work is scheduled to take place on the third or fourth Monday of every month. As they were returning, they received on the car radio a message that this escape was taking place after I report that Lentz and Daly had just stolen one of Aubrey West's small pickup trucks and was driving it away. Jim do not forget under normal GHVSP procedures an alarm and an APB goes out inside and outside PDQ. My report will be correct and the only five people that will know the alarm and report are false will be you, me, the Chief and of course my two guards.

Charles, I like your plan its simple foolproof and will work but I am still not a big believer in cold blooded murder. Jim I can understand that but these two men are walking dead men here inside or outside. It's away of life they selected and continue to pursue, what else can we do we have to play the game? OK, Charles call, the Chief and let's get the ball rolling and put your plan in place. Hello, hi Peg This is Charles is the Chief in. Yes, he is, Chief it's for you! Hello Charles. Chief Jim and I have my "Some Way" Escape Plan for Lentz and Daly ready to present to you when can you see us? Hell, you fuckin AH it's about time get your asses up here let's put it in place and make it happen. Great we are on the way.

April 19,1939. Wednesday morning about 1030Hr Jim and Charles are seated in the Chiefs office as they present to him in detail Charles's Escape Plan involving Doug Lentz and Frank Daly. About an hour later Charles completes his presentation and asks the Chief what he thinks? Charles, I like it, using your two security guards in the mix the way you did makes it foolproof plus they do all the dirty work. I am sure it will convince the Chief VSBI Agent Sean Nuttycombe that it was a legit escape attempt by two desperate men. That should keep that AH and his hoods off of our backs. Let's go with it Charles, let it be said and let it be done. Well Chief if you or Jim do have any more questions let me go and get the ball rolling. As Jim leaves, he tells Peg meet me at the car in about thirty minutes.

Chapter 8

SIMPLE ESCAPE PLANS FAIL

April 19, 1939. Wednesday about 1200Hr Peg gets in Jim' car and they drive slowly downs Lolly Dolly Road. As expected, their entire conversation is to discuss Charles Escape Plan for Lentz and Daly that Charles is putting in place as they chat. Jim I am very worried what if this escape plan fails. If it does this whole fuckin GHVSP will go down the tubes and heads will fall and roll. I know my dear but rest assured nothing like that will happen this escape plan is so simple and foolproof. I certainly hope you are right, working here is bad enough but to be knowledgeable of planned escape murders is hard for me to except. I realize that Peg but like Charles said these two inmates are walking dead men either inside or outside as free men. Do not forget the fact that they shot and killed two innocent police officers in cold blood in Norfolk, Virginia that had young families. Peg, look at it this way, it's up to the Good Lord to meet and forgive them, our job is to just set up this meeting!

April 24, 1939. Monday morning about 0700Hr Jim is in his office sipping on a cup of hot coffee just thinking and staring up at the ceiling. Peg is at her desk in the Chiefs office sipping on a cup of hot cup and also just thinking and staring at the ceiling. Both she and Jim realize this is probably the worse, day of their lives as they are through no part of their own involved in the cold blooded murder of two young people whether they are guilty or not. All they can say is God Forgive Us For What We Do!

The Chief finally comes in about 0730Hr. He seems to be in a serious but happy mood as Peg quickly gets him a cup of hot coffee. He grins and tells Peg this is a big day stay loose as this place is going to look like Grand Central Station in New York City before this day is over, Big Money in the bank for the GHVSP Slush Fund. Peg just thinks, does this greedy cruel AH have any compassion; all he thinks about is himself and how much money he has. April, 24, 1939. Monday morning it is now about 0745Hr as the GHVSP Security Force Guard Sargent (Sgt) Clifton Ewell comes to Holding Cell No. 201 to get inmates Douglas Lentz and Frank Daly and march them to their work detail duties at the GHQM. As they arrive at the mine entrance Charles has Sgt Ewell separate Lentz and Daly from the other detail Inmates. He then marches them over to a lone Aubrey West Mine Co. Pickup truck parked nearby and tells them to back the truck close to the mine entrance rail cars and unload the miscellaneous supplies from the truck to the mine rail cars and take the truck back and park it where they found it. As they do this Charles as planned leaves them alone and discreetly walks back to the Administration Building and up to the Chiefs office to report the planned escape and the stolen truck when it takes place and to wait for the final results of his planned escape to be reported by Security Force guard Patrick Payne.

As instructed earlier inmates Doug Lentz and Frank Daly park the truck out of sight and quickly pull on the Aubrey West Mine Co. coveralls that nicely covers their GHVSP uniforms, then put on the Co. hard hats. They quickly get back in the Aubrey West Co. pickup truck and drive off slowly over too and around the outside prison wall driveway to the GHVSP Main Gate turn left and drive straight down Lolly Dolly Road. Doug looks at Frank and grins; SOB old buddy this is going to be a piece a fuckin cake. Frank as he drives asks Doug where are we going? Who knows and who gives a shit as long as we get out of this fuckin GHVSP Hell Hole? Well Doug you know what the old man always says? No. what did the old man say? He said, "if you do not know where you are going. You will sure in hell end up somewhere else that's for damn sure"! Both Inmates Doug and Frank laugh like hell, now that's funny. Shit Frank you are so full of BS I bet you could make "Pigs Fly", HA, HA!

As they slowly drive down Lolly Dolly Road towards Rt 250 Frank asks Doug what did that note from prison trustee Henry Johnson say that he slipped in your food tray this morning? Holy shit Frank I have been so excited I forgot about that note. SOB, Doug you fuckin AH he whispered to you for us to read it right away then tear it up, good luck and be very careful. SOB, Frank here it is as he quickly opens a small envelope and removes the note. Well, AH what does it say? Holy Shit Frank it reads, "Be careful you may be driving in to a trap or set up of some kind. Under the seat you will find a small box! You both owe me $50 each, cash only I do not take checks, HA, HA!" Doug what the hell does all that BS mean? Who knows? Well AH get the fuckin box and let's find out. Doug reaches under the truck seat finds, removes and opens the box. SOB, Frank it contains two cheap revolvers and an extra box of cartridges. Here Frank, take one revolver and be prepared to use it if need be. Old Henry Johnson is no fool and he knows something is going down that's for damn sure.

As Frank approaches the Rt 250 intersection he slows down to stop as he sees two GHVSP Guards step out of an unmarked GHVSP car. Doug looks over at Frank and says they are right on time just like Captain Stanton told us. As the two guards approach the truck carrying a small box each Frank watches them closely. One guard appears to be very nervous and locks and loads his rifle. Why would he do that? As an experienced Carbone Mafia Cartel "Hit Man" Frank shouts out loud to Doug it's an ambush its a fuckin trap, shoot their fuckin asses and let's get the hell out of here. Both Frank and Doug duck down as they quickly open the truck doors and fire away an take out both GHVSP Guards Patrick Payne and Russell Rice. Just to make sure they are dead they calmly walk over and shoot each one between the eyes. SOB, Frank that was a close call, old Henry Johnson will get his turkey that's for damn sure plus $100 cash for these two old revolvers. Here Doug let's clean out their pockets and put their dead asses in the truck. What are you going to do? Same old shit as we have done in the past. Good idea as Frank rips the shirt off of one of the dead guards. With both dead guard bodies now loaded in the truck he twists the shirt tightly up into a fuse and forces it tightly down the truck gasoline fuel fill spout. He quickly lights the fuse off as he and Doug run like hell and jump in the unmarked GHVSP car and drive West on down Rt 250. Holy Shit Frank when that fuckin truck with a full fuel tank explodes those two AH; the Chief Warden Foster and Captain Charles Stanton are going to shit in their pants. I hope so you have to believe those two SOB set us up for some reason.

April 24, 1939. Monday morning about 0930Hr escaped GHVSP inmates Frank Daly and Doug Lentz continue to drive

West on Rt 250 towards Staunton. In the distance behind them they hear the explosion they have been listening for. SOB Frank did you hear that? Doug I sure did, music to my ears I just bet that whole damn GHVSP shook. As they continue to ride along, they listen to the two way radio in the car speak to their escape. APB are being announced describing the two escaped inmates as being armed and dangerous and driving a 1936 Ford four door unmarked GHVSP sedan; Virginia License No. "GHVSP 1". This car is believed to be heading East towards Richmond on Rt 250. Well Doug my old buddy there you have it we are back in the limelight once again. Well Frank what do you think we ought to do first? Well first thing we need to do is get rid of these coveralls and prison clothes, then this car or at least replace the license plates.

Much later still driving down Rt 250 West well out of Staunton Frank is getting tired and decides to pull into the Old Beautiful Bright Sommerville Waterfall Attraction, Lodge and Restaurant. It's a small Mom and Pop facility that is clean, nice, quiet and out of the way type of place. As Frank parks the car he tells Doug let's take our chances and check in here and stay a few days and just let the dust settle for a while. What about our clothes? Well, if anyone says anything for now just tell them we work for Aubrey West Mining Co. and are in town doing some contract work over at the Dolly Ramsey Draft Granite Mine. As for the car license plates just smear a little mud on them for now. Later after dark I will slip over and steal those plates off of that old deserted car setting sitting next to that big trash bin. OK, let's go and check in and get something to eat my fuckin stomach thinks my fuckin throat is cut. Frank one last thing before we go in; reload your revolver. If we should get unexpected visitors, we have no choice but to shoot our way out I can tell you I am not going back to that dreaded GHVSP for any reason you can bet your sweet ass on that. Doug, you check in as Patrick Payne and I will check in as Russell Rice we have their wallets and drivers licenses if we should need identifications for any reason.

April 24, 1939. Monday morning about 0930Hr back at the GHVSP as expected there is nothing but mayhem and wholesale panic!!!!!! The Chief Warden Foster and Security Force Captain Stanton are at the Rt 250, Lolly Dolly Road intersection (Now considered a major crime site). Rescuer vehicles are at the site along with extra GHVSP Security Force Guards. As they all survey the site little or nothing remains but ashes. The explosion and devastation of the Aubrey West Co. truck has almost vaporized everything. The Chief and Charles are in total disbelief as Assistant Wardens Erma Kersay and Jason Mitchell come quickly driving up. They are bringing expected news that the VSBI are sending Agents up to investigate that will include VSBI Chief Agent Sean Nuttycombe; ETA 1600Hr this afternoon. The Chief thanks Erma and Jason and tells them he will call them later for a special meeting in his office to go and just stand by for now.

As the Chief and Charles realize there is nothing more they can do here at the crime site they get in their car and drive back to the Main GHVSP Complex. The Chief asks Charles what the fuck happened I though your plan was foolproof? Chief it beats the hell out of me, Lentz and Daly must have gotten inside help from someone. Well, we need to come up with some damn good excuses quick that fuckin Sean Nuttycombe is going to be on our ass like flies on a pile of cow shit!!!!! Meet me in my office about 1300Hr, Nuttycombe and his fuckin snoops are expected here this evening around 1600Hr and we need to be prepared for them.

Chapter 9

ON THE RUN WHAT NEXT

April 24, 1939. Monday afternoon about 1300Hr Charles, Erma, Jason, Jim and Peg are seated in the Chiefs office. They say nothing and of course all are somewhat sad about the turn of events. The Chief opens the meeting by stating that a tragic occurrence took place at this GHVSP this morning that costs us the lives of two loyal Security Force Guards; Patrick Payne and Russell Rice. These two men were murdered in cold blood by two escaping inmates Doug Lentz and Frank Daly. These two inmates are now on the run somewhere still in this State we believe between this GHVSP and Norfolk, Virginia driving a stolen GHVSP unmarked car. An APB has been announced that speaks to this and that is all we know at this time. I feel deep down inside they had inside and outside help from the Carbone Mafia Cartel in order to put their escape plan in place. If any of you know or have heard anything please speak up. Confide in your Prison Trustees and see what they might know or have heard and be prepared to be thoroughly questioned by the VSBI investigators when they arrive later today.

Peg just sits in her chair behind her desk and bites her tongue. What a brilliant speech by the Chief loaded with a ton of his usual BS. All of these greedy bastards are members of the GHVSP "Special Five" but she and Jim. Peg knows all the where, what and why facts involved but like Jim her hands are tied and they are both locked in and only have one avenue out of this mess and that is to just up and leave. The Chief looks around and states if no one knows anything or has anything to say at this time I consider this meeting to be complete and over. I advise you all to go back to your office and put your stories together based on times and places as the VSBI Agents will be asking you this along with other questions. Just be prepared and remember, no one can rest or feel safe until these two murders are captured.

April 24, 1939. Monday afternoon about 1645Hr a knock comes on the Chiefs office door as Peg gets up to let the expected VSBI Agents in; Chief VSBI Agent Sean Nuttycombe and two of his Agents Tracey Leyden and David Sikes. Everyone knows each other from past meetings over the years and formal introductions are not necessary. The Chief Warden Ken Foster and Captain Charles Stanton welcome them all with cordial and sullen greetings as Peg gets everyone a hot cup of coffee. Chief VSBI Agent Sean Nuttycombe opens the investigation meeting by stating Ken what the fuck happened up here? How did something like this even take place, a clean prison break from your escape proof GHVSP that's never succeeded before? Sean, Charles and I do not have a clue. Lentz and Daly by blowing up that truck they stole did not leave us any clues of any kind, nothing! Yes, Ken we realized that as we stopped at the crime site briefly when we drove in. Sean, Charles and I believe it was set up by the local Carbone Mafia Cartel working out of Norfolk. You realize the local Mafia Cartel "Don" Harrison Paul Daly is the uncle of escapee Doug Lentz and the father of escapee Frank Daly. Yes, Ken we know about all of the family history and connections. It's an unfortunate connection for Agent Dave Sikes sitting here to be in as he is engaged to Betty Daly, Harrison Paul Daly's only daughter and sister of escapee Frank Daly. The Bureau has no problems with this as investigations prove Betty has no Mafia connections of any kind and has been estranged from her father and the whole Daly family for years.

Sean we cannot explain this escape; it was so well planned and was over before we even discovered it. Charles had these two inmates under a strict security watch 24/7 as you requested. How they were able to steal that Aubrey West Co. truck and drive off unnoticed beats the shit out of me and Charles. Chief have you questioned any of your staff and the prison trustees to see if any of them have heard, seen or know anything that may help us? Sean as we speak my Assistant Wardens Lt Jason Mitchell and Lt Erma Kersay and Security Force Captain Charles Stanton have these investigations going on. As soon as I receive these full reports from them in the next few days I will I send them to you right away.

Well Ken it looks like you and Charles have things here pretty much under control. All I can say is whoever helped these two inmates escape did an excellent planning job. Its obvious from my experience that they received inside and outside help. Ken I can see there is not a lot my VSBI Agents and I can do here so I will just leave this investigation in your hands and the hands of your GHVSP Staff. Sean, are you leaving now? Yes, just send me all your complied reports for review and file ASAP the VSBI Director Guy Chapman will be expecting those. As for now I want to get back to the crime site and look around some more before sunset. Ken every crime site always leaves evidence of some kind. If these two inmates had inside and outside help which I am sure they did, we will discover it we always do.

Well Sean, like I said we will continue to investigate here at our end and keep you posted. Ken, I know I can rely on you and your excellent staff here at the GHVSP to do a complete job. Ken you and Charles must realize the importance we were placing on the hopefully verified testimonies of these two escaped inmates. If these testimonies could have been obtained and verified as expected it's a chance, we could have brought down the local Carbone Mafia Cartel and it's "Don"; Harrison Paul Daly. Ken we must locate and keep Lentz and Daly alive and safe. Sean, you have to realize these are two dead men walking. Family or not the Carbone Mafia Cartel and Harrison Paul Daly want them eliminated ASAP.

VSBI Chief Agent Sean Nuttycombe and his two Agents Tracey Leyden and David Sikes finally leave as Peg gets up and locks the door behind them. SOB Charles I sure did not expect Nuttycombe's visit to be that short or polite. Let's face it you can tell this escape is not important to him as it was well planned and carried out. What's important to him is the capture of Lentz and Daly alive and getting their testimonies nothing else matters. Charles, do you have any idea where they may be headed? Well under normal escape plans they would travel to Norfolk and seek protection from the Feds by the Carbone Mafia Cartel. However, if they heard the Carbone Mafia Cartel knew they were going to go "Yellow Canary Bird" and sing they would haul ass in the opposite direction PDQ. Chief who ever helped them here inside must have tipped them off that the Carbone Mafia Cartel knew about their VSBI testimony plans and wanted them eliminated. Hell Charles, who inside here could have possibly known about that Carbone Mafia Cartel Note but you, Jim, Peg and I. Shit Chief how the fuck would I know, my guess is they got tipped off some how and are driving West not East.

April 26, 1939. Wednesday morning Doug Lentz and Frank Daly are up early. They both having completed their triple "S" put on clean civilian slacks and "T" shirts they purchased used at the Deerfield Volunteer Department Thrift Store. As they safely sit, chat and eat breakfast in the quaint old Bright Sommerville Lodge Restaurant Doug asks Frank how much money do they have remaining? Frank reaches in his pocket and removes a small roll of cash and counts it. Doug all toll counting what the two guards had and what we had saved from our highly paid prison salaries $245. How much do you have? Frank I only have $6.

Well Frank what do we do next, we cannot just stay here we need to move on, $251 is not going to last us very long? Well Doug I have been looking at a Roadmap I picked up in the Lodge Lobby and thinking. We, only have a few choices; one lay low in this area and sign on with the Dolly Family Mine Co. and go to work for them at their Reddish Knob or Ramsey Draft Mines, both are close by. Frank fuck that mining BS I have had enough mine work to last me a fuckin lifetime. Well, choice two, continue to drive West on Rt 250 across the West Virginia State Line to WVA Rt 28 and head on over to Beckley and go to work in one of their Coal Mine Co. as outside truck drivers. Hell, Doug do you have any suggestions? Frank do not forget we are two heavy marked men and based on these daily APB everyone in Virginia and West Virginia is on the lookout for us. I am thinking to be safe we can still speak to the VSBI and see if they still have a Federal Witness Protection Program

Contract, they will offer us. Doug are you fuckin crazy? Well Frank we cannot continue to be on the run forever. Sooner or later the Carbone Mafia Cartel or the VSBI will run us down and we will be killed in a shootout or returned back to a Penitentiary for life once again. Well, if you want to give it a shot there is a telephone in the Lobby go for it. Doug do not forget we have murdered four Law Enforcement Officers in cold blood. Yes Frank, I realize that but I also realize the Carbone Mafia Cartel wants us dead and the FBI and VSBI want us alive. Shit AH go make the fuckin telephone call. Here take half of this money and keep it just in case we get separated.

April 26, 1939. Wednesday morning GHVSP escapee Doug Lentz is in the Bright Sommerville Lodge Lobby to make a long distance collect telephone call to the VSBI Main Field Office in Richmond. Finally, the local Augusta County telephone operator Nancy Diaz has success and the call goes through. A nice young lady answers the telephone and excepts the collect call. Sir this is the VSBI Main Field Office in Richmond, how may I help you? Young lady what is your name? Jennifer. Jennifer is this a secure telephone connection? Yes sir, it is! Well in that case please let me speak with VSBI Chief Agent Sean Nuttycombe. Yes sir, let me connect you with his office. Hello Chief Agent Sean Nuttycombe speaking who am I speaking with? Mr. Nuttycombe this is Doug Lentz. Who? Doug Lentz! SOB Lentz we are searching all over for you and your Buddy Frank. No shit, are you tracing this call no you are secure no traces and no party lines. Well, I am calling to see if Frank Daly and I can still meet with you somewhere close by and discuss a Witness Protection Program Contract with you, is that still possible?

Lentz I am not sure that's possible now, we had it all set up but you two AH pulled off that GHVSP escape and in doing so murdered two prison guards. Hell, we had no choice they were about to murder us as we were ambushed and set up. Holy shit, who set you up? It was an inside set up I will discuss with you when or if we meet. OK Lentz let me discuss your telephone call with the VSBI Director Guy Chapman and call you back. Lentz give me a telephone number I can reach you on? No sir I will call you back tomorrow morning at 1000Hr. OK call me direct Person to Person on my secure telephone line, TP No. 5-1919. Got it click!

Doug feeling somewhat safer and relieved walks back to the restaurant and sits down in the booth with Frank. Franks looks at him and says did you talk to the man with the big bright red fuzzy nuts? Yes, I certainly did, well you AH what did he say? He would not commit all he would say is he will discuss it with his boss VSBI Director Guy Chapman and check back with us. Holy shit I hope you did not give him our location here at the Lodge? Hell no, you dumb shit, I told him I will call him tomorrow morning about 100Hr.

Chapter 10

AMBUSHED AND MURDERED

April 27, 1939. Thursday morning Frank and Doug go to the Bright Sommerville Lodge Restaurant early to eat breakfast. Doug completes his breakfast and tells Frank you stay here I am going to the Lobby and make my planned 1000Hr telephone call to VSBI Chief Agent Sean Nuttycombe. Doug goes to the Lobby, quietly looks around and quickly slips in the telephone booth and places his Person to Person Collect telephone call to TP No. 5-1919. The call goes straight through. Hello VSBI Chief Agent Nuttycombe. Chief Nuttycombe Doug Lentz here what do you have for us and make it quick? Well, I spoke with our VSBI Director Guy Chapman; he spent several hours with the Virginia State Attorney's Office. Based on such short notice and the severity of your crimes they said they cannot guarantee a complete Witness Protection Program package for you two guys at this time. Nuttycombe what the fuck are you talking about it sounds like you are just blowing smoke up my ass.

Lentz any Witness Protection Program package we offer you, will still require some substantial incarceration time but it can be reduced to a lesser sentence than life and provides a chance for parole and later outside protection and placement. Lentz that's it, I can bring this Witness Protection program contract to you and go over it with you. If you agree to meet with me, I will be required to arrest you on the spot and bring you back and incarcerate you both in our VSBI Prison Barracks. There you will remain until a Three Judge Panel decides on your case and on your final sentencing guidelines. After sentencing you will be incarcerated in a minimum security prison to serve your time until you are finally paroled and released. After you are released, you will be sent to an undisclosed small town unknown to anyone with all new falsified identification papers and some new facial disguises it you wish. That's it, Lentz take it or leave it. I suggest you take it ASAP; it sure beats the hell out of a one way drum boat ride out on the Chesapeake Bay. Nuttycombe it's not what we had expected or had in mind. Let me run it by Frank and call you back later! Click!

Doug somewhat disgusted goes back to the Lodge Restaurant and sits down with Frank and discusses the Federal Witness Program Package VSBI Chief Agent Sean Nuttycombe presented to them. As they sip coffee both of them come up with all sorts of "What Ifs". In the end they realize they have ruined their lives getting involved with organized crime and now must pay the consequences and take what is offered in order to survive. A safe holding cell in a minimum security prison like Nuttycombe said sure beats the hell out of a drum boat ride out on the Chesapeake Bay or a shoot out on a lonely street corner somewhere. Frank looks at Doug and says shit Doug go call Nuttycombe back and tell him to show up here alone with a Criminal Lawyer that will speak on our behalf and notarize the Witness Protection Program contract signatures. Doug goes and makes the telephone call and returns back to the Lodge Restaurant and orders more coffee. Frank it's a done deal, Nuttycombe, one of his VSBI Agents as required and a VSBI Criminal Lawyer will meet with us tomorrow afternoon at 1300Hr at the Deerfield Volunteer Fire Department to review the contract they will offer us. He will take care of all the arrangements. He said for us to be prepared to be arrested and taken at that time back with them to Richmond to be officially listed as captured and incarcerated.

April 27, 1939. Frank and Doug complete their breakfast and get ready to leave the Lodge Restaurant when they notice that two Augusta County Sheriff's Deputies have come in and are sitting in a booth across the room from them. One of the Deputies looks over at them and nods then continues to drink his coffee and chat with his buddy. Finally, one of the Deputies gets up and walks over to speak with Doug and Frank. Frank is very uncomfortable with this as he nods right to Doug. Doug knows that means for him to cover the right side should a confrontation take place. Both realize this maybe it. Doug concentrates on the seated Deputy while they talk with the Deputy that has confronted them. The Deputy smiles and puts out his hand to shake and says my name is Bran Poe that's my partner over there Marvin Clay. You two fellows are new in town where are you coming from? Doug introduces himself as Patrick Payne and this is my work buddy Russell Rice, we work for Aubrey West Mine Engineering Company out of Carrisbrook we are in town TDY to support some contract work for Mr. Dolly at his Ramsey Draft Granite mine. SOB, I have not seen Mr. Dolly in a while how is he doing? He is doing just fine just old and cranky as shit. Hell that old fucker was that way when he was a kid!

Well, nice to have you both in town if you need anything just let us know. I hope I did not upset you in anyway by checking up on you but everyone around here is uncomfortable as two notorious killers are running loose that escaped from the GHVSP and word has it they maybe in our neck of the woods. No problem, Bran you are just doing your job. Well fellows it seems like all strangers these days are persons of interest (POI). Like I said Pat and Russ if you need anything just give us a holler as he walks off to his booth and sits down. Doug looks at Frank and says what do you think? Doug, I think he was just doing his job but he did seem a little nervous. Well lets slowly get up and get the hell out of here.

April 28,1939. Friday afternoon about 1230Hr Frank pulls into the large parking area of the Deerfield Volunteer Fire Department and as a cautious move backs the car up to the close by woods that border the property and parks. He and Doug check their revolvers to make sure they are fully loaded. They make sure the coast is clear then get out of the car and walk into the woods behind the car and hide. As normal for most volunteer fire departments no one is on duty full time as most of the volunteers have full time outside jobs and come running only when an alarm is announced or when called on otherwise.

It is now about 1330Hr as Doug whispers to Frank I had a feeling that fucking Nuttycombe was stringing me along, that fucker is a no show. About that time an Augusta County Sheriffs car pulls up to the Fire Department front door office. Two Deputies get out and go inside; would you believe they are Bran Poe and Marvin Clay. Frank and Doug still well hidden keep their eyes glued to the office door. Frank this does not look good, this may be another setup. The Fire Department door opens and the two Deputies walk out and over towards

Frank and Doug's car. Doug and Frank quietly listen as Bran tells Marvin this is definitely the stolen GHVSP car it matches our report. As the two Deputies start to open the car door and begin a search another car drives up to the Fire Department front door and parks. The two Deputies pause and Bran looks at Marvin and says who the fuck can that be I do not recognize the car? How the hell would I know maybe it's the VSBI Agents that the local telephone operator Nancy Diaz told us about that planned on driving up from Richmond to meet with those two GHVSP Escapees. We better walk over and check them out, if its them we can let them know they have been stood up. (Flash Back: Remember Nancy Diaz placed Doug Lentz's long distance telephone call to VSBI Chief Agent Sean Nuttycombe).

As the two Deputies start to walk over to the car that just arrived VSBI Agents Sean Nuttycombe, David Sikes and VSBI Agent Criminal Lawyer Winston Kerr step out of the car and walk towards them. Not hearing Deputy Marvin Clay mention Nancy Diaz telling them about this meeting; Frank tells Doug your fuckin trusted buddy Nuttycombe has set us up this is a fuckin trap. Well Frank like I said I am not going back to that Fuckin GHVSP hell hole we have no choice and we have to do what we have to do!!!!!! Frank you take out the two Depos, I will take out the three VSBI Agents, let's do it. Frank and Doug quietly step out of the woods and hide behind their parked car as the five men walk towards their car. As the five men get close well within point blank range Frank hollers go and they fire away. All five of the very surprised men are dropped and are killed that quick. As Doug walks around to make sure they are all dead. He walks over to Nuttycombe; Nuttycombe in his last breath whispers to Lentz it was the local telephone operator that tipped them off not me, we could have made a deal with you. Doug looks at Frank with a blank stupid look on his face and says too late now, Shit Happens. Frank lets drag these five fuckin dead AH in the woods and get the hell out of here before anyone else shows up? OK, let's collect their wallets before we leave we can always use the cash money, let's go. As Frank drives off he asks Doug where too? Doug says Beckley West Virginia as he reloads their revolvers. Doug do you realize we are going to set a new State of Virginia Record! We are, in what event? The Murder One Category, it is now up to nine. All of our Victories have been Law Enforcement Victims. Not really one of those AH was a Lawyer Ambulance Chaser. Hell I forgot about that. Shit we did everyone a favor when we eliminated that crooked AH. Frank I think the judges will give us credit for him as he was considered a VSBI Agent. Well in that case the record still stands at nine and we still get the "GOLD". How nice!!!

April 28, 1939. Friday evening about 1800Hr two volunteer firemen Martin Barnes and Larry Fuller drive up to the Volunteer Department front door and park next to the two parked cars already sitting there. They go inside and look around, no one in sight. Hell Marty where can they be the Deputy Sheriffs car belongs to Bran and Marvin we know that. Hell, knowing them two they probably had friends pick them up to go get a gut bomb somewhere and look for some gals they both stay horny and they are always looking around for BB&P.

April 29, 1939. Saturday morning early, Augusta County Sheriff Lee Metz comes driving into the Deerfield Volunteer Fire Department parking area and parks right next to his County Deputies car and the VSBI car. He is very upset with Deputies Bran Poe and Mervin Clay for leaving the car unattended overnight and not reporting in to the office as required. He has his only other Deputy Billy Marks with him. He tells Billy to take care of the dogs while he goes inside and jumps in volunteer fireman Martin Barnes shit for not reporting both car locations.

Sheriff Metz the cars have only been here overnight and they have not been officially reported as missing by anyone that I know of, besides that Deputies Bran and Marvin are in and out of here all the time. By the way where are they? No one knows we have not seen them or the owners of the other parked car. Well Larry and I stayed here overnight and we figured all these folks would show up late last night and pick up their cars, as you can see that did not happen. Hell Sheriff do not come in here jumping in my shit just because you cannot keep tabbs on your two little boy scouts and their fuckin beer drinking buddies. Marty I am sorry and very upset, trying to support this County with just three Deputies and myself is getting to be too much of a job for me, I think it's time for me to hang it up and just get the hell out of dodge.

April 29,1939. Saturday morning still at the Deerfield Volunteer Fire Department Deputy Billy Marks comes running inside the office front door all excited and upset. Sheriff Metz you and Marty better come with me quick. I let Riley and Sarah our two dogs out of the car to relief themselves and they ran in to the nearby woods. They started barking, I checked them out and they have discovered a terrible gruesome sight. Sheriff it is terrible. All three men walk back in to the woods a short distance to view the terrible sight Billy was telling them about. It is horrible as they have discovered the deceased bodies of five men. Two of course they recognize as Deputies Bran Poe and Marvin Clay and the other three are of course VSBI Agents Sean Nuttycombe, David Sikes and Winston Kerr all unknown and new to them.

Holy Shit Billy all five of these men have been shot at close range and murdered in an ambush. Sheriff how can you tell that? Billy, small bore bullet holes and all their weapons are still in their holsters unfired. It happened so fast they never had a chance to reach for, draw or fire a gun. Sheriff what are we going to do? Billy it's nothing we can do but go back in the office and telephone the VASP and the VSBI and notify them on what we have discovered and let them take over. Something this serious and professional is certainly out of our hands. Billy put the dogs back in the car while I go inside and make these telephone calls. This is going to be one sad day for the people of Augusta County; Bran and Marvin were two fine local boys born and raised right here in the County.

Chapter 11

INSIDE OUTSIDE HELP

April 29, 1939. Saturday afternoon about 1300Hr GHVSP Chief Warden Foster is sitting over at his desk working his ass off doing nothing as usual but listening to his scanner. As he listens he hears the APB announcement that speaks to the tragic ambush that took place sometime yesterday at the Deerfield Volunteer Fire Department parking area in Deerfield, Virginia. As all family members of the murder victims have now been notified the VSBI is releasing more details. These details describe what may have occurred including the names of the five murder victims. As the Chief hears the names of VSBI Chief Agent Sean Nuttycombe and two of his VSBI Agents David Sikes and Winston Kerr he gets a sinking feeling deep down inside. He knows at times he had negative feelings about Nuttycombe but never the less he realizes the State of Virginia has lost a fine hardworking Law Enforcement Officer along with two other fine young Agents, Sikes and Kerr.

About this time GHVSP Security Force Captain Charles Stanton comes walking in to the Chiefs office along with T/CPA Jim Rawls Jr and his secretary Peg Vinsen all just returning from lunch. SOB Chief, did you hear the tragic news about Nuttycombe, Sikes and Kerr? Yes I just heard the APB on the scanner report. Those no good fuckin murders Lentz and Daly are nothing but born killers and we should have eliminated them here inside months ago. God only knows we sure had many chances to do so that's for damn sure. Peg sits at her desk weeping as Jim walks over to comfort her as he has a good idea why she is upset. She realizes if she or Jim had only come forward with just one secret telephone call they would have possibly saved the lives of five to seven young men. Dear God Forgive Us?
   Chief what can we do? Charles there is nothing we can do. These inmates confined in here are serving long prison terms and have nothing to lose. They will as expected stick together through hell and high water and most of them have some kind of outside help from friends in low places. Peg shakes her head and thinks to herself; Chief you had better include yourself and the rest of the GHVSP Special Five. Charles I can tell you this, inform your Security Force Staff to tighten things up around here and stay lose especially Assistant Wardens Kersay and Mitchell. Sad news of this kind only encourages these inmates to think, if Lentz and Daly can pull this off maybe they can too, maybe it's time to make a move. Folks like I said there is not much we can do, so it's business as usual. I just hope and pray that these two killers Lentz and Daly are apprehended very soon before they can kill again.
   April 28, 1939. Friday evening late escape GHVSP inmates Lentz and Daly drive in to the Clarion Lodge and Restaurant Beckley West Virginia parking lot and park. It's a quiet Mom

and Dad type of place well off the beaten path. They check in, Doug Lentz as Patrick Payne and Frank Daly as Russell Rice. Both are tired out from the long drive. They quickly complete their triple "S" and go back to the Restaurant to eat a late supper. As they eat they strike up a friendly conversation with a few of the locals who like most of the folks that live in that area work in the Coal Mines. One young feller John Ensley tells them living here you have two choices; you either work in a coal mine or you pack up and leave. HA, HA! Well John we do not want to leave can you suggest a Coal Mine Co. that would hire two old truck drivers like Pat and me? Hell yes Russ, the Old Archer Coal Mine Co. just up the road about a mile from here. I have a supervisors job there. Drive over there Monday morning about 0700Hr and they will put you to work right away. Tell them John Ensley sent you, if you do that I receive five extra Archer Mine Co. tokens. They give those out for every men I/we recruit, HA, HA! No problem Big John thank you for the information, can we buy you a cold beer? You sure can, don't mind if I do!

May 01, 1939. Monday morning about 0630Hr Patrick Payne and Russell Rice drive over to the Old Archer Coal Mine Co. and like Big John Ensley said they get hired right on the spot as Mine Rail Car Drivers. It's a dirty job as expected but it beats the hell out of a swinging a sledge hammer all day crushing granite stones in a fuckin prison Quarry mine. Later that evening Doug asks Frank what do you think about our jobs? Hell we better not complain at least we are working and off the beaten path. Let's just cool it for a while and see what takes place and play it by ear.

May 12,1939. Friday morning about 0800Hr Peg walks in to the Chiefs office and drops several large mail envelopes on her desk. One of these catches her eye right away as it is from the VSBI Director Guy Chapman. She quickly opens it and finds out it contains VSBI Chief Agent's Sean Nuttycombe's final report that speaks to the Lentz and Daly Escape Crime Site. To paraphrase the report it states that the crime site was so devastated that nothing could be found to present any real clues or evidence of any kind to support what might have taken place. The badly burned skulls of Guards Patrick Payne and Russell Rice were recovered. Both of these indicate one bullet hole shot at point blank range using a small bore gun of some kind. The only way Lentz and Daly could have received these guns was from inside and outside help. Who supplied these guns and this help? Peg thinks to herself that question may never be answered but she would put her money on Prison Trustee Old Henry Johnson. GHVSP rumors speak to him as the go between man inside if you need anything and let's face it he was a very good friend of both Lentz and Daly.

About 1230Hr Jim calls Peg and tells her to meet him at his car so they can go to lunch at Phills Pub as usual. Peg does this and as she gets in to the car Jim throws a small envelope containing a note on the seat and tells her to read this. Peg I picked that up out of my Blue Bird House pick box up this morning. The note reads; The Carbone Mafia Cartel wants Douglas Lentz and Frank Daly located and eliminated ASAP. The Gratuity will be doubled once this is accomplished, you people make this happen you blew the fuckin planned escape now fix it. Also we know that these two received inside help. Find these persons that furnished this inside help and eliminate them also.

May 12, 1939. Friday about 1400Hr Peg now back from lunch is sitting at her desk waiting for the Chief to return. At about 1430Hr the Chief walks in and sits at his desk and says to Peg; Peg I think I have had enough of this fuckin GHVSP for one day. I think I will take the rest of the day off and just go to Phills Pub drink a few beers and just go home and rest. Chief before you leave you might want to read this before you go. Jim passed it on to me at lunch it's from the Carbone Mafia Cartel he picked it up this morning. After reading the note the Chief tells Peg call Erma, Jason and Charles and have them report to my office PDQ. About 1500Hr Erma, Jason and Charles come walking in to the Chiefs office. Realizing from the tone of Peg's voice on the telephone they know it's serious and of course want to know what's up. The Chief passes the note around for all of them to read. Folks we just received this from Jim he just gave it to Peg to bring to us. I told you earlier there was nothing we could do, as you can see that has changed. Well Chief where do we start? Charles I want you three to put a plan in place. Charles I suggest you start with your Security Force Guards who mainly work the Holding Cell Blocks and see who comes and goes. Be very careful as the inside help many of these inmates receive may come from one of your guards after all they come and go everyday unchecked. After all your Guards have been cleared and recertified then start with your Prison Trustees. I know for a fact a lot of these Prison Trustees are very friendly with the inmates they serve each day bringing them food trays and of course their mail. Erma do not rule out any of your female Prison Trustees just because they are isolated and work the female Holding Cell Blocks. It is now May 12,1939. I will expect full reports from all of you working together on my desk the morning of May 19, 1939.

    Chief working with the entire GHVSP population inside is all well and good but how do we go about locating Lentz and Daly and eliminating them as stated in the Mafia note? Folks all we can do is listen to all reports, read all the newspapers and by all means keep your scanners on to receive all APB reports.

Lentz and Daly are professionals at what they do. They know the Carbone Mafia Cartel wants them dead and they also know from APB broadcasts that all Law Enforcement Agencies in Virginia, West Virginia, North Carolina and Kentucky are all on full alert searching for them. Chief I understand what you are saying and fully agree but what do we do to get involved and get Lentz and Daly when captured, released to us? Erma all we can do is sit back and take a wait and see approach. If and when they are captured hopefully alive we present a plan that will convince the arresting parties to release them over to us. If we cannot arrange that we lose a large gratuity payment from the local Carbone Mafia Cartel. Chief I know these two killers very well and they will never be captured alive. If we find them first and take them out it will be shit house luck. Charles I hate to say this but I feel you are correct, but anyway keep your eyes and ears open. Folks that's all that I have, go and start your investigations on your Guards and Prison Trustees and get your reports back to me ASAP.

May 19, 1939. Friday morning early Peg comes in to the office early carrying the mail. Three plain envelopes containing the expected investigation reports from Erma, Jason and Charles arrive. As allowed and trusted to do so Peg sits down at her desk sips coffee and begins to slowly read each report and outline major things of interest. The report from Assistant Warden Jason Mitchell contains a statement related to his conversation with his Guard Sgt Roy Runyon. It states in part that he has noticed Prison Trustee Henry Johnson spending a lot of extra time here lately each morning chatting with both of the escaped inmates Lentz and Daly when he delivers their Food Trays. In addition he delivers a lot of their mail even though Prison Trustee Rubin James is the appointed and assigned mailman for their Holding Cell Block. All of the mail deliveries usually take place after the inmates have left on their work details. When Rubin James delivers the mail he is in such a hurry he usually just throws it inside the Holding Cell on the floor. When Henry Johnson delivers the mail to Lentz and Daly he carefully reaches in the Holding Cell and places it face down on a small tray. Sgt Roy Runyon told me he has never given much thought to this until I questioned him this past week about possible inmate support from outside sources. Jason in his report goes on to say he had conversations with both Prison Trustees James and Johnson who are good friends and also share the same Holding Cell. Rubin James told him that Henry Johnson does deliver the mail at times for him when he is running late and well behind or for other reasons. I ask him why Henry Johnson when he delivers the mail he places it face down? Rubin James said it's just a habit Henry has, plus he has the time. He said he does not have the time to do this so he just tosses it inside as he is in a rush to report to the Main Mail Room. Guard Sgt Roy Runyon has assigned him with extra duties in the Mail Room to sort out standard mail while he opens and inspects incoming packages. Rubin James told me please do not fault Henry Johnson he is a true friend and a big help to him and he can assure me Henry Johnson is not helping anyone inside or outside of this GHVSP. To quote Rubin James; he said my Guard Sgt Roy Runyon is the AH causing mail delivery problems and holdups and that I needed to get him off his lazy ass and make him do his job and work harder. I told Rubin James I would look into the problem and get them more help.

May 19, 1939. Friday morning about 0900Hr the Chief finally shows up. Peg brings him a cup of hot coffee and tells him you sure are running late this morning plus you look like shit, HA, HA! He laughs and gives her the finger. Chief I put the Investigation Reports from Erma, Jason and Charles on your desk. Great Peg they got them here on time as requested, did you review them yet? Yes I did but I still want to check them over more closely. The only one that really speaks to a problem is the one from Jason and it just involves an in house mail delivery problem. Chief Guard Sgt Roy Runyon along with help from Prison Trustee Rubin James inspects and sorts out all of the mail going and coming this includes all packages. Chief let's be realistic to actually smuggle weapons of any kind in to this GHVSP it would have to be done by someone on your staff that comes and goes on a daily basis. Peg you are probably correct Erma, Jason and Charles need to keep a closer watch on their people there is a nigger in the coal pile somewhere.

Chapter 12

BOTH GHVSP ESCAPEES LOCATED

May 20, 1939. Saturday evening GHVSP Escapees Doug Lentz (a.k.a. Patrick Payne) and Frank Daly(a.k.a. Russell Rice) are sitting in the Clarion Lodge Restaurant sipping on a few cold beers. They are in a happy mood as they continue to enjoy their tragic and ill gained Freedom from Justice. They have steady jobs with good pay at the Archer Coal Mine Co. now working for Supervisor Big John Ensley who they consider a good boss and friend who treats them well.

Having just received their pay in cash and tokens before they left work, Doug tells Frank to give him $50. You want $50 from me what the fuck for? Yes, I am going to mail it to Prison Trustee Old Henry Johnson at the GHVSP to pay him for his help and the two guns he provided for us. Doug are you serious? Hell yes! Frank that old nigger saved our lives we owe him that much, he put his head on the chopping block for us. Damn Doug how do you plan to do this? You do realize your letter will be Post

Marked Beckley, West Virginia. Yes I know but I will put my letter and the money to Henry Johnson in a small envelope and send it to his Holding Cell mate Prison Trustee Rubin James in another envelope, Holding Cell No. 100. Rubin James will receive it directly as he works in the Main Mail Room sorting mail. He will take it to Henry Johnson unopened, unseen and untouched, no problems. OK Doug if you say so but I sure hope you are not stepping on your fuckin dick. Frank you worry too much. Doug you seem to forget we are highly sort after GHVSP Escapees. Doug the latest APB offers a cash reward of $10K for our fuckin asses "Dead or Alive". All these fuckin West Virginia Hillbilly's in this town are searching for us, $10K will buy a ton of B B &P. Frank let me give you some fuckin advice; keep your beard, let your hair grow long, talk the talk and walk the walk. No worry, Frank calm down and let me buy us another beer.

May 29, 1939. Monday morning early Frank and Doug report in to work at the Archer Coal Mine Co. Later as they take a cigarette break outside the mines main entrance Doug reaches in his pocket and finds the letter to Rubin James he forgot to mail this morning. Hell Frank I am going to run over to John Ensley's office and drop off this letter I will be right back. As he walks in the office John's secretary Paulet Britt looks up and says good morning Patrick can I help you? No hon, I just need to drop this letter off in the outgoing U.S. Mail box here on the wall. Hell Pat just throw it in that box full of mail on the table over there I am getting ready to make a Mail Run in to town. Great will do, done deal, thank you! Right after Pat leaves Paulet puts on her coat, grabs her purse and picks up the full box of mail and gets ready to leave. As she does this she notices Patrick's (a.k.a. Doug Lentz) letter on top and the strange forwarding address on it. It reads; To Mr. Rubin James GHVSP Apt 100, Carrisbrook, Virginia. As she puts the letter back in the box her Boss John Ensley walks in. Still curious about the address on Pat's letter she picks it up and tells John here check out this address. SOB Paulet where did you get this? Patrick Payne just dropped it off. Paulet let me keep it and do not say a word about it to anyone just keep it between you and me. No problem John, let me run. Where are you going? In to town to make my weekly mail run. Hell do you mind if I ride with you? Not at all what's wrong? I am strongly curious about that letter it needs to be opened and checked out and Sheriff Williams office is in the same building next to the U.S. Post Office, let's stop in and show it to him. Paulet to be on the safe side he can legally open it and review its contents. It may just contain a friendly note but I have a hunch its more involved. Just for the record get Patrick Payne's and Russell Rice's Archer Co. Employee Records and let's take them along with us, we may need them.

May 29, 1939. Monday afternoon about 1230Hr John Ensley and Paulet Britt knock on the door of the Beckley City Sheriff's office. The sheriff Floyd Williams shouts come on in the door is always open. As they walk in the sheriff looks up and says John Ensley you old SOB how are you, long time no see and who is that beautiful lady you have with you? Willy this is my right arm Miss. Paulet Britt. You all please come in sit down and let me get us all a fresh brewed cup of coffee. What brings you to my humbled abode, things around here are really quiet? Willy I have a problem, it's just a hunch and I maybe making a mountain out of a mole hill but I want you to officially open this letter and check out its contents. As John hands sheriff Williams the letter he explains his reasons to him and describes Patrick Payne's and Russell Rice's actions and their sudden changes in appearances to him. Sheriff Williams reads the forwarding address on the letter and then carefully opens it using a sharp letter opener. John if it contains evidence to support your suspicious reasons we need to keep it in place and intact, if not we can put the contents in a new envelope and just mail it on out at the Main U.S. Post Office next door as if it's been untouched. As the Sheriff removes the contents, a $100 bill and a brief letter. The Sheriff reads the letter out loud and it reads; Henry thank you and Rubin for your support, spend the gun payment money wisely. Tell Captain Charles Stanton his ass is grass and I am the fuckin lawnmower and his ass will go up in flames. SOB John just reading this letter I am not sure I fully understand it's full meaning but I can sure tell you this; from my many years in the Law Enforcement business you probably have the two most notorious wanted men in the U.S.A. today working for you at the Archer Coal Mine Co. Shit Willy what can I do these two men will kill in a moment's notice if confronted? I know! We need to be very careful and not tip them off in anyway. You and Paulet return back to work as usual. I will set up some apprehension plans for these two and keep you updated. John here, before you leave let me call Charles Stanton he is the Security Force Captain at the GHVSP and verify the information we have read in this letter and let him know we are pretty sure we have located his two GHVSP Escapees. John I will put the telephone call on my new telephone speaker system so you and Paulet can hear and speak also. Willy do you know Charles Stanton? Hell yes, I trained the little AH. Hell he worked right here in this office for five to six years. I have his home and business telephone numbers right here on file.

May 29, 1939. Monday afternoon it's now about 1400Hr as Beckley Sheriff Floyd Williams makes his long distance telephone call to the GHVSP to contact Captain Charles Stanton. Hello GHVSP telephone operator who is calling? Operator this is Beckley West Virginia Sheriff Williams I would like to speak with Captain Charles Stanton. Yes Sir, let me put you through to his office. Hello Captain Charles Stanton who is calling? Charles you AH it's your old boss Floyd Williams! SOB Willy, how in the hell are you doing? Hell, I was just thinking about you the other day and wondering when you were going to hang it up and retire. You old AH you must be about a hundred years by now! Are you still fucking your secretary Linda Peabody every day? Hell me and the rest of your trainees years ago said if we had a nickel for every time we caught you with her ass bent over your old oak desk fuckin her eyeballs out we would need a fuckin truck to carry them all to the Bank, HA, HA! Charles will you knock the BS off, I am calling you on a very serious matter and besides that I have two other people on my speaker telephone system. Oh shit Willy I am sorry! SOB, Willy please forgive me? Sir, please state your business? Charles I am sitting here with Mr. John Ensley and his beautiful highly embarrassed Secretary Miss. Paulet Britt. We are sure we have located your two GHVSP Escapees Lentz and Daly and that they are working for Mr. Ensley at our local Archer Coal Mine Co. Here is what we have so far and I need you to verify this before I notify the West Virginia State Police (WVSP) and have them set up Apprehension Plans to capture these two known killers. Holy Shit Sheriff we need to get these two killers off the street ASAP, go ahead and give me what you have. As the Sheriff reads the Lentz letter, Charles tells him right off Sheriff you got them they are definitely our two escapees. Well Charles like I said we were pretty sure but we wanted to call you to verify and confirm. Sheriff Williams here is what I would like you and Mr. Ensley to do for me if you will and can? Do not do anything but continue working and acting normal around them so as not to tip them off in any way. Just let me and some of my GHVSP Security Force people drive over and make the arrest of these two and bring them back here. Once we have them back here me and Chief Warden Ken Foster would like to interrogate them for information related to Inside and Outside support help from the local Carbone Mafia Cartel. After that is complete we will then turn them over to the VSBI and FBI for new formal charges to be placed. Once this is done I can tell you this they will never see day light again. Sheriff can you take care of this for me? Yes Charles I believe so, but it is not normal State Guideline Procedures. If something goes wrong my ass will be in some very deep hot water. Sheriff do not worry I know these two very well and I can assure you nothing will go wrong. OK if you say so, but before I let you go Mr. Ensley has a few questions to ask you.

Mr. Ensley nice to meet you sorry it has to be under such horrible conditions. Same here Charles. Charles do you have any idea when and where you will arrest these two killers. John I will start my plans right away and let you and the Sheriff know what they are when I have them complete. I can tell you this it will not be at your place of business. All I need from you is information related to these two i.e. Work hours, Residence addresses and locations, Car make, model, license No., telephone No. etc. Charles we can give you all of that now as Paulet has their Archer Coal Mine Co. Employee Records right here. We anticipated this. Great give this information to me now and we can get these two killers off the street ASAP, let's make it happen. OK, let me put Paulet on she has the files already open and in front of her. Hello Mr. Stanton this is Paulet Britt speaking do you have a pen and paper ready? Yes Miss. Britt I do but before we start let me apologize to you for my lewd opening telephone remarks. I had no idea Sheriff Williams had you two folks on a telephone speaker system. No worry Charles, working for the Archer Coal Mine Co. I have heard it all. My

Dad told me if you work with men you learn to talk like men; if it can be said it can be read. Charles you are the lucky one; if you had been here instead of talking on the telephone Sheriff Williams would have shot your fuckin ass between the eyes! SOB, Miss. Britt you are my kind of gal. Sheriff Williams and John Ensley laugh and go down for the count! OK Charles here is the information you will need and want: Lentz (a, k, a, Patrick Payne) and Daly (a. k. a. Russell Rice) live full time at the Clarion Lodge and Restaurant located at 6108 Jefferson Highway, Apartment and combined Kitchenette No.100. They drive a 1936 four door Green Ford Sedan, VA License No. 200. They both have beards and extremely long hair. You should have the rest of their profiles on your GHVSP Files. Charles that covers what I have, any questions? No Miss. Britt you have covered all the bases thank you. Miss. Britt if you get a chance to come this way give me a call on this number, I would like to meet you and show you around. Yes I just bet you would! Charles just get yourself an old oak wood desk and a pretty young secretary and bend her over the desk every day, you do not need me! Like I said Miss. Britt you are my kind of gal you got me back big time. As they all laugh at how Paulet handled herself; Sheriff Williams says Charles all joking aside keep us posted and make this thing happen these two killers are not stupid and they are looking over their shoulders all the time as all known killers do. Sheriff tell me about it you ought to be working here full time. No worry sir, me and my men will be on the way ASAP. Thanks to your training years ago I know just what to do and will set it up.

Chapter 13

ESCAPE NUMBER TWO SUCCEEDS

May 29, 1939. Monday afternoon about 1530Hr Security Force Captain Charles Stanton calls the Chief Warden in his office and tells him to call the other staff members to his office for a short meeting that he has received some very good news related to escapees Lentz and Daly from Sheriff Floyd Williams in Beckley West Virginia. The Chief very excited has Peg make the calls PDQ. About 1545Hr Erma, Jason, Charles And Jim are all seated in the Chiefs office. Peg as usual secures the door and pulls down all the interior shades. The Chief looks at Charles and says; Charles it's your call go for it and open your meeting.

Everyone is anxious, as Charles tells them that the two GHVSP Escapees Lentz and Daly have been located in Beckley West Virginia employed and working full time for a Coal Mining Company. Believe it or not they are using the names of my two Guards they murdered Patrick Payne and

Russell Rice as aliases and are still driving the same unmarked GHVSP car they stole at the same time. All this information was just telephoned to me by one of my old Bosses Sheriff Floyd Williams in Beckley West Virginia. Sheriff Williams with some reluctance will honor my request and stand down and let us here at the GHVSP drive over and arrest these two killers if I can get your approval. I have already put some plans in place but I still need your input, advice and like I said your approval. Charles what are you plans I would like to help you, as Pat and Russ were two of my best friends. Thank you Jason!

Well this is what I would like to do! I would like to drive myself and one of my Guards, Sgt Roy Runyon over to Beckley tomorrow morning early and meet with Sheriff Williams and discuss my plans with him, pick up the letter he read to me and other evidence he may have. That letter clearly indicates that Prison Trustees Henry Johnson and Rubin James are the persons inside the GHVSP that supported their escape. After that I want to drive over to the Clarion Lodge and check out the residence where Lentz and Daly are living. Charles all of this is well and good but what is your basic apprehension plan? Well on Wednesday morning May 31, Roy and I dressed in typical coal mine coveralls will walk around the Clarion Lodge and closely check out the Combined Apartment and Kitchenette No.100 where these two killers are living full time. If things go as normal they will be at work. On June 01, the next day we lay in wait and ambush them both early when they come out to go to work, done deal! We of course plan on shooting them both down on sight. Remember Jim's note from the local Carbone Mafia Cartel speaks to a double Gratuity when we eliminate them. Later as planned, the Pollock Funeral Home in Carrisbrook can pick the two bodies up at the local Beckley City Morgue. The VSBI $10K Reward money "Dead or Alive" will of course go to the Archer Coal Mine Employees John Ensley and Paulet Britt that intercepted Lentz's letter and took it to Sheriff Williams. That was the tipoff that set this whole thing up. Any questions, any advice or input? Yes Jim! Charles just make sure you pick up Lentz's letter and money to Henry Johnson (via) Rubin James and bring it back here. I can tell you the local Carbone Mafia Cartel will want to see and get a copy of that. Also make sure you collect their guns and squeeze off a few rounds to make your ambush appear as a legit shoot out to satisfy the West Virginia Law Enforcement Investigating Teams. Charles just cover your tracks well because once this shoot out is reported the story will be in every newspaper in the U.S.A.

May 30, 1939. Tuesday morning at the crack of dawn GHVSP Security Force Captain Charles Stanton and one of his Guards Sgt Roy Runyon in an unmarked GHVSP car, both dressed in Coal Mine Coveralls are driving on their way to Beckley, West Virginia. Late that afternoon they finally arrive at the Beckley Sheriff's Office. Charles parks the car and they walk right in. As they meet Sheriff Williams he looks up and cannot believe how much his young trainee Charles Stanton has changed, it's been so long. Charles gives him a big hug and says Willy you look worn out. Charles I really am, I have had enough of this Law Enforcement Racket and just this week filled out and submitted my retirement papers. Good for you, you have worked long and hard all your life; it's time. Willy this is one of my main GHVSP Guards Sgt Roy Runyon. Hi Roy nice to meet you! You guys sit down while I get us all a fresh brewed cup of hot coffee and we can get started reviewing your plans.

May 30, 1939. Tuesday afternoon Charles and Roy are still in Sheriff Williams office as they continue to discuss Charles apprehension plans involving Lentz and Daly. Charles your plan appears safe and foolproof to me lets go with it. By the way where are you two guys staying. Willy I think we will check in at the Clarion Lodge and Restaurant, always dress like this and stay low and out of sight. I think by doing that we should be safe enough. Well maybe so as our reports indicate Lentz and Daly stay well confined in their room and eat all their meals in their kitchenette. Well that's all I have, Willy do you have any advice? Yes, lock and load, stay out of sight and shoot to kill. YES SIR! Here Charles do not forget this, it's Lentz's Letter to Rubin James.

May 30, 1939. Tuesday evening late Charles and Roy drive over to the Clarion Lodge and Restaurant and check in. After checking in they go over to the Restaurant for a much needed supper. In the meantime Doug Lentz and Frank Daly are in their Clarion Apartment No.100 just finishing up supper. Doug looks over at Frank and says I am going to run over to the Lobby and buy some cigarettes I am just about out do you need anything? No Doug just stay low and be careful. As Doug buys his cigarettes he walks by the lobby door leading to the restaurant and stops to read the daily food meals menu they have posted. He glances in the restaurant and just about has a heart attack as he sees Captain Charles Stanton and Guard Roy Runyon in a nearby booth eating supper. Holy Shit he says to himself as he hauls ass back to his Apartment. Out of breath he tells Frank you are not going to believe this but GHVSP Captain Charles Stanton and one of his guards Sgt Roy Runyon are sitting in the restaurant eating supper. SOB Doug, something big is going down this is no consequence they must be here searching for us, somehow we have been exposed. SOB Frank this might be it, what can we do? Well for one thing just calm your fucking ass down and let me think for a minute and put some defensive plans in place. You have to believe they know we are here and my guess they will may make a move probably tomorrow May 31, or no later than June 01. Doug the big defense we have is the fact they are here and do not realize we know this.

Doug here is my plan if you can think of anything different speak up? Tonight late pull our car around back and park it right by our back door. We pack up all of our things and put them on the back seat of the car and be set to get the hell out of here PDQ. My guess Charles and Roy will quietly come by tomorrow, see the car gone, think we are at work and just walk in to our apartment unannounced to search it for guns etc they know we have. Not knowing how long they have been in town my guess they will be lying in wait for us to return from work and make their strike at that time. What we need to do is get up early and hide here and wait. You can hide behind that big chair over by the wall and I will hide behind the kitchen curtain. When they walk in feeling safe and relaxed and start to look around Doug you quickly grab your buddy Charles Stanton from behind and crack his skull open using one of these cast iron skillets here on the stove. At the same time I will grab Roy Runyon and do the same thing. We make sure they are dead and load their dead bodies in the car trunk out back and slowly get ready to leave, done deal no noise a perfect ambush. Doug you drive our car and follow me. I will steal that new 1939 Buick parked next door I have been looking at and head on down Jefferson Highway. About a mile down on the left is an old road leading down to the closed and abandon Beckley land fill. Drive in there behind me and we can pull over at a lonely spot and park. Then what? Damn you AH business as usual. OH shit not again, why not? We stuff a Lodge towel in the car gas tank fill spout light it off as a fuse and slowly drive off. Frank you are a fuckin genius.

May 31, 1939. Wednesday morning very early GHVSP Escapees Doug Lentz and Frank Daly are busy putting their escape plan in place. Their car is out back fully loaded. They take their hidden places in the apartment as discussed. Finally after a long wait they hear the door being unlocked and as expected Charles Stanton and Roy Runyon walk in as if they own the place. Doug as planned grabs Charles from behind and with no problem cracks his skull with the heavy cast iron skillet. Frank easily does the same thing to Roy. SOB that was much easier than I expected. Here Doug lets collect their wallets and guns we can use the cash later and the guns too if need be. As Frank goes through Charles pockets he pulls out Doug's letter addressed to Rubin James. Doug look at this it's your fuckin letter to Rubin James. You dumb SOB I told you that fuckin letter may get us in trouble. Somehow Charles Stanton received it and was tipped off we were here. Too late now let's just load these two bodies in the car trunk and get the hell out of here.

As they finish loading the two bodies in the car trunk Frank tells Doug to drive around and meet him out front I am going to go next door and take that new 1939 Buick I have it already set up to steal, no problem. Just as they get ready to finally leave the front door suddenly opens and in walks Beckley Sheriff Floyd Williams. As luck would have it he is acting alone as a self appointed backup. SOB talk about being in the wrong place at the wrong time; Doug and Frank quickly overpower the old man and like the others bash his skull in and load him in the car trunk with Charles and Roy. SOB Frank let's get the hell out of here before we have any more surprise visitors.

May 31, 1939. Wednesday morning about 0600Hr Frank drives down Jefferson Highway in his brand new 1939 Buick. After driving for about a mile he turns left on to the old dirt abandon road leading down to the now closed Beckley City landfill. He looks back and as planned Doug is right behind him. He laughs as he passes a big "NO TRESPASSING SIGN", hurt me. About a mile down he finds a secluded spot and turns around. Doug pulls up beside him stops and they quickly reload their personal items from the old Ford to the Buick. That done Frank for safety reasons drives further down the road and parks and walks back. Frank looks at Doug and says; talk about a God forsaken place, hell it will be months before anyone drives in here and finds what is left of this car. Frank you are right let's do the deed and move on. Frank pulls an old towel out of his pocket. He twists it tight and forces it down the gas tank spout of the old 1936 GHVSP Ford car. A perfect fuse, he lights it off and he Doug run back jump in their new 1939 Buick and drive off. As they get back to Jefferson Highway they stop and listen for and hear the expected explosion. SOB Frank do think there is anything remaining? Doug I doubt it remember we topped off the gas tank yesterday just in case, HA, HA!

As they turn South and drive down Jefferson Highway Frank tells Doug you got your wish! I did what was that? You said Charles Stanton's ass was grass and you was a fuckin lawnmower and his ass will go up in flames. SOB Frank you are right, by the way do we still hold the "Murder One Law Enforcement Record" yes indeed and it's up to twelve. SOB! By the way where are we headed? Biloxi Mississippi we have some friends there in low places. Sounds good to me "Scratch Gravel White Wing" and put her ass in the wind.

Chapter 14

WHAT HAPPENED WHERE ARE THEY

June 02, 1939. Friday morning the Chief is sitting at his desk. He looks over at Peg and says I wonder why Charles Stanton has not telephoned us? He said he was planning to make the apprehension of Lentz and Daly early on the morning of June 01 when they came out of their Clarion Lodge Apartment to go to work. Chief I do not understand either, I certainly hope there were no snafu's or foul ups. Peg I doubt that, Charles and Roy had this too well planned out, a perfect ambush. Chief do you want me to telephone call the Beckley Clarion Lodge and check on them? No not yet they may have altered their plans let's wait until later. If we have not heard something from them by 1400Hr call the Beckley Sheriff's Office and get a update from Sheriff Williams.

June 02, 1939. Friday about 1430Hr the Chief tells Peg to make that call to the Beckley Sheriff's Office he has a strong hunch Charles and Roy have had some problems. Peg has good luck and her person to person telephone call goes straight through. Hello, Beckley Sheriff's Office Linda Peabody speaking how may I help you? Linda this is Peggy Vinsen in Carrisbrook, Virginia at the GHVSP calling on behalf of Chief Warden Ken Foster; he would like to speak with Sheriff Williams if he is available. Peg I am sorry to say, but Sheriff Williams has not been in the office since early Wednesday morning. All I can tell you is he left me a note telling me he was going over to the Clarion Lodge on Jefferson Highway on business to support two folks from your place; a Mr. Charles Stanton and a Mr. Roy Runyon. Peg I am not sure what the business was all about as I just got back from being on vacation and I am trying to get caught up. Willy was in such a hurry when he left he as usual did not tell me anything. Lord Linda I know exactly what you mean; "They will not let you touch the throttle, blow the whistle or ring the bell, but let the fuckin train jump track and see who catches Hell"! Peg you got that right. Peg I am worried to death about him. His Dear Wife Eddie Mae has been calling all over checking on him as he did not check in with her or come home Wednesday night. For some unknown reason no one has seen or heard from him. Linda we are having the same problems with Charles and Roy they have not checked in with us as discussed. Peg we only have two other deputies working in this office and both of them are out of town on vacations. Peg I am upset and I am not sure what to do next or tell you at this time. Peg let me do this, after I hang up talking with you I will call Willy's wife, if she has not heard from him by now I will call the West Virginia State Police (WVSP) and talk with Bubba and have him check in on this problem and call me back. Peg it may be awhile as the University of West Virginia Mountaineers are playing double hitter baseball games in town today and both WVSP Troopers always make sure they are on duty at those games. Linda I understand, I will just sit tight and wait for your telephone call, you have our direct GHVSP operator number? Yes I sure do! Good bye Linda, thank you.

June 02, 1939. Friday about 1530Hr Peg tells the Chief about her telephone conversation with Beckley Sheriff Williams secretary Linda Peabody. Peg none of this sounds good, I have a strong gut feeling that something very serious has taken place. Three well trained and experienced Law Enforcement Officers all unofficially missing at the same time, no way? Chief I have the same feeling. Peg if we do not hear anything from Linda Peabody or the WVSP by quitting time today can you possibly come in and work overtime tomorrow? I realize it's your weekend off but I have a very important meeting in Richmond, Virginia at the Virginia State Penitentiary on Spring Street I really need to attend. I know I have it scheduled on my daily log. No problem Chief, one of us needs to be here to receive Linda's call. I think about Charles and Roy and I am very worried about both of them.

June 03, 1939. Saturday morning early about 0700Hr Peg reports in to work as requested, hoping to receive some good news from Linda Peabody. She checks her daily and weekly schedule and log. With that taken care of she decides to clean up the office some and just get rid of some junk on the Chief's desk and finds a letter partially hidden in a dictionary. She is curious as she normally sees all the mail before the Chief does but for some unknown reason the Chief received this letter directly and it by passed her. Being all alone she has the time and starts to read this private letter and finds out right away it was sent special delivery from the Virginia State Treasurer Wesley Howard. The letter briefly states; I received your list of concerns in your letter to me dated April 14, 1939. As I do not want to respond to them in writing I will research your request and speak with you in person in Richmond at our yearly meeting on June 03, 1939. Wes! Peg thinks about the words of this letter and just writes it off for now and returns the letter back to where she found it.

It's now about 1200Hr as Peg is just sitting quietly reading and sipping on a cup of coffee when her telephone rings. Finally after many anxious hours of waiting she picks up and it's her return call from Linda Peabody. Hi Linda good news I hope? Well Peg, not really the local WVSP Captain Bubba Buxton just left as he was in a hurry to go on duty at another Mountaineer baseball game. However he did drop off a brief report speaking to his investigation on the disappearances of Sheriff Williams and your two folks Charles Stanton and Roy Runyon. I will paraphrase my response to you on the telephone and send you a copy of the full report ASAP. Bubba's report reads; that he could find no evidence that any crimes have been committed at the Clarion Lodge and Restaurant. The car of Sheriff Williams was found completely intact and parked right next to it was your GHVSP Car license No. GHVSP 2 also intact. No signs of the three missing men could be found. A search of the two escapees Apartment No.100 indicates no problems and was clean and neat as a pin. However they of course as expected could not be found and your GHVSP car license No. GHVSP 1 (VA 200) was not to be found. A telephone call to the Archer Coal Mine Co. reported Lentz and Daly did not report into work Wednesday morning or since as required. Bubba just stated it appears that all five men have all of a sudden just vanished in to thin air. He has of course as required issued a APB related to these disappearances. Peg that's all that I have. I am worried sick and I do not know what else to do or tell you at this time. Deep down inside I just know something terrible has taken place but no evidence can be found to support my feelings. You and I know three experienced Law Enforcement Offices do not just disappear into thin air. Peg I will keep you posted if I hear anything else, please do the same? OK Linda, thank you I sure will, good bye!

June 03, 1939. Saturday about 1400Hr. Peg still in her office at the GHVSP realizes with great sadness there is nothing more she can do calls Jim and tells him to meet her at Phills Pub for a late lunch. As they relax and chat Peg tells Jim about her conversation with Linda Peabody. He just grins in a sad way and states; Peg greed is a terrible thing. Charles wanted to capture and murder Lentz and Daly in a planned ambush so the GHVSP Special Five could get full credit and receive the Local Carbone Mafia Cartel Gratuity. My guess Lentz and Daly got lucky and spotted them and in some way took them out. I am sure the ambush table got turned around. Peg if they have not reported in by now forget it they are history where ever they may be. Charles and Roy should have stayed out of this apprehension set up and let the West Virginia Law Enforcement Authorities handle the arrest of these two as it fell under their Jurisdiction in its entirety not ours. Like Mom always said; you can lie, cheat and steal but it will always come home sooner or later. I warned Charles and Roy the morning they left for Beckley, West Virginia to be extremely careful as they may end up fighting fire with fire as these two killers Lentz and Daly have nothing left to lose and are not stupid.

Jim I am so tired of my job and this GHVSP way of life, I just want to get away from it all. Peg my dear bear with me a little longer my plans for us are falling into place. Jim you keep telling me this, when are you going to discuss these plans with me? Soon my dear very soon. Peg I just had a good idea; let's forget all our worries for now, go home, drink some merlot wine, take a hot shower, get shit faced, hop in the rack, play doctor and fuck. My bad boy is telling me it's pie time at the "Y" and it's been awhile. Great idea James, let's go nurse Jane herself is beginning to bubble like a hard crab.

Chapter 15

ELIMINATE JOHNSON AND JAMES

June 05, 1939. Monday morning about 0700Hr Peg unlocks the GHVSP door to her and the Chiefs office. She is humming, happy and satisfied after spending a very restful and sexy weekend with her little Jimmy. She and Jim spent a lot of time discussing future plans together as he told her about most of the plans for them he had in place. She is overwhelmed but like he told her they all must remain their secret for a short while longer. She checks her daily schedule and log and calls the GHVSP operator to check on any incoming long distance calls. Nothing, that dulls her happy feelings as no news from Beckley, West Virginia means bad news still lies in wait somewhere.

About 0900Hr still half shit faced the Chief walks in. Damn Chief you look like shit! Hell Peg I feel like shit to much Jackie Dee will surely fuck you up. How did things go Saturday any word? Yes, but not good as she gives him her brief on the telephone report she received from Beckley Sheriff Williams secretary Linda Peabody. SOB, Peg after reading this and not hearing from Charles or Roy by now you have to believe the worse for them has taken place. Sooner or later something has to show up good or bad. As reality is sinking in Peg begins to weep, Chief I sense you are correct I doubt we will ever see or hear from Charles or Roy again. Peg my gut feeling is the same. Peg I hate to sound harsh but we still have a Penitentiary to run, we have to except and expect the worse has occurred and plan for the future. Please call Jason, Erma and Jim and tell them to report my office by 1030Hr. Yes sir will do!

June 05, 1939. Monday about 1030Hr Jason, Erma and Jim are all seated in the Chiefs office. Peg as usual secures the door and pulls the interior shades and gets everyone coffee. All are sadden as the Chief updates them on the latest bad news from Beckley related to their two good friends and coworkers Charles Stanton and Roy Runyon. Folks we have to except the loss of these two men and plan for the future, life goes on. Jason as of this moment I am promoting you take over Charles position as our new Security Force Captain. You of course have a major problem right off as you have lost four security force staff members over the last few months. I will trust your judgement on who you will promote to fill your position. As some of you might know I attended an important meeting in Richmond this past weekend with one of our Special Five members, the State Treasurer and he answered most of our questions I sent him on April 14,1939. I will review these with you at our quarterly meeting here on July 07, 1939 at 0900Hr, any questions. Yes Jim! No questions just a statement; folks in your June 30,1939 gratuity envelopes your cash payments will be greatly reduced but it's the best I can do based on our sources of supply. Folks if no questions I consider this meeting adjourned. I will keep you updated if and when we receive any reports speaking to

Charles or Roy. Jason please remain as I need to discuss a few things related to your new position in private. Jim and Peg as I would like to speak to Jason in private, now would be a good time for you to take your lunch break. Chief we understand, Peg grab you purse and lets run over to Phills Pub and get one of his famous Gut Bombs. Jim lets go I am ready!

June 05, 1939. Monday about 1200Hr Jason sits quietly as he already knows what questions the Chief is probably going to ask him. As the Chief secures the door and sits down he looks Jason straight in the eyes and says what are your plans for eliminating Henry Johnson and Rubin James. We know from escapee Doug Lentz's intercepted letter that Henry Johnson and Rubin James helped him and Frank Daly escape. Also we have a nice Gratuity of $200K from the Local Carbone Mafia Cartel waiting for us once we reveal their names and eliminate them as requested. Chief I am not sure how to eliminate them and make it appear as an accident. Do you have any ideas? Hell Jason just set it up using our "Big Lake", "SHE" method. I thought about that but both of these men have been incarcerated for over thirty plus years. They are 100% Institutionalized and this prison way of life is all they remember and have ever known, why leave? Chief they have it made living here safely inside; room and board, medical care and as Prison Trustees get the full run of the place. Even if we let them escape unharmed where would they go? These inside inmates are the only family they know. Jason the only way we can receive that Carbone Mafia Gratuity is to eliminate them and make it appear as an accident so come up with some method to eliminate them and just make it happen quick. OK Chief let me think some more and I will get back with you ASAP. Please do!

June 07, 1939. Wednesday evening about 1600Hr newly promoted Security Force Captain Jason Mitchell comes barging in to the Chiefs office unannounced. He is excited as he loudly tells the Chief he has a plan that will help them eliminate Henry Johnson and Rubin James. The Chief is very disturbed as he wanted all of this kept a secret between him and Jason. Too little too late as Peg looks over at them and they realize she has heard every word Jason said. SOB Jason, why don't you just announce your plans to the whole fuckin World and put them in the Local Newspaper. Sorry Chief, I fucked up! The Chief looks over at Peg! Peg nods, puts her finger over her mouth, shushes and says mums the word Chief I did not hear a thing. Business as usual, no worry! Thank you Peg. Peg knows it's time to leave gathers her things and leaves to go home for the night. As she leave she nods and says I will see you tomorrow. Goodnight! After Peg leaves the Chief walks over and locks the door and looks at Jason and says; OK Big Fuckin Mouth lets go over your elimination plans and they better be damn good!!!!!!!???? Well tomorrow Aubrey West is going to move a large amount of dynamite from his big storage area that is locked behind the Red Door in the "Big Lake Cavern". He needs this dynamite to blow up granite he wants to start processing from the Southern Branch of the Cavern.

Chief in doing this he has requested we let him use about four GHVSP inmates along with him and his son Aubrey West Jr to do this moving work. As usual he will use GHVSP Mine Rail Cars. Jason this is routine how does this involve Henry Johnson and Rubin James? Chief these four inmates working with Aubrey West will miss their normal supper time breaks. So as a normal procedure I will have Prison Trustees Henry Johnson and Rubin James deliver their supper food trays to them at the work site. Henry Johnson and Rubin James will trailer these food trays from the kitchen to the GHQM entrance and transport them by mine rail car right to these inmates on site. No problems as they have done this many times before.

Chief here is where I make my move. My Guard Sgt Clifton Ewell and I will remove a small section of rail tracking at the switch off that goes down to the seldom used "Big Lake" branch of the Cavern. When Henry Johnson and Rubin James strike that fouled up switch track the mine rail car they are driving easily jumps track and tumble down the adjacent steep roadway and roll in to the "Big Lake". Henry Johnson and Rubin James strapped in by seat belts will sink with the mine rail car and of course drown an accidental death. Sad to say but this will appear and be reported as another GHVSP mine accident. SOB, Jason that is a Perfect Elimination and Accident Plan.

Chief I sure feel bad about this as Henry Johnson and Rubin James to be prison inmates are two very nice guys. I will miss them as they have been a lot of help to me and our whole GHVSP staff over the years. Hell Jason shit happens and do not forget those two killers that Henry Johnson and Rubin James helped escape murdered two of our best Guards, Patrick Payne and Russell Rice. Shit Jason you will get over it when you drive to the Bank to deposit your slice of that big Carbone Mafia Cartel Gratuity. Jason when will all of this happen? Tomorrow June 08, between 1700Hr and 1800Hr. Great, as I want to make sure I am not at the GHVSP when you report this accident. Chief where will you be? Over at Phills Pub getting shit faced, call me after you officially report the accident. By the way Jason where will you be? Well to make sure the accident occurs as planned I thought Sgt Clifton Ewell and I would stay on site and just help Aubrey West load dynamite. Aubrey told me it's a big job and will take a while.

June 08, 1939. Thursday morning Peg is at her desk about 0700Hr when the Chief walks in. SOB Chief what brings you here so early are you lost? HA, HA! Peg keep talking like that and I might have to fire your beautiful fuckin ass! Hurt me and make pigs fly! Peg what do you have on your daily log for me today? Nothing special, just make your usual rounds and piss people off, things are beginning to settle down. Still no word on Charles and Roy. Well let me get going and make my rounds there are one or two AH I need to kick in the ass and a few names I need to take. Peg I will be leaving early today I have a hot date this evening with Nan Hart do you know her? Know her, shit Chief I heard she has been in the rack with just about every single guy in Carrisbrook. Peg do not be so nasty she is a nice girl. Chief nice girls put it in for you, HA, HA! Peg, you are really on a roll today; let me go.

As the Chief begins to leave his office Jim walks in. Good morning Chief, what brings you here so early, did you get lost? HA, HA! Very funny Jim did you come to see me or just to do standup comedy with your girlfriend. No I just need to talk with Peg for a minute. Good let me go! As the Chief finally leaves Peg gets Jim and her a cup of coffee. She looks at Jim and says what is wrong? Peg this sealed note was inside my desk draw when I opened it this morning. Here read it and let me know what you think? Peg takes the note and reads it. It simply reads: Prison Trustees Henry Johnson and Rubin James are the two insiders that helped Doug Lentz and Frank Daly Escape. Security Force Guard Sgt Clifton Ewell is the outsider that assisted them. Jim where do you suppose this note came from? Peg all I can tell you is I have friends in "Low Places"!!!! Peg do you think I should pass this note on to the Chief Warden? No not really he already knows about Henry Johnson and Rubin James being involved and I am guessing he now knows about Clifton Ewell. Peg I can tell you this the Local Carbone Mafia Cartel is willing to pay a Gratuity of $100K each for the location and elimination of these three if it appears as an accident. Damn Jim, $300K that's a lot of money. Tell me about it!

Jim my dear I think we may be able to earn most of that Gratuity on our own and not even become involved. Peg what the hell are you talking about? Well last night before I left to come home our newly promoted Security Force Captain Jason Mitchell came in the office all excited about a plan he had put together to eliminate Prison Trustees Henry Johnson and Rubin James. Peg how do you know about this? I heard him make that statement before I left. Instead of leaving as the Chief expected I just stepped outside the locked office door unseen and listen to the Chief and Jason discuss the plan. Jim if I heard things correctly Henry Johnson and Rubin James will be eliminated in a GHQM drowning accident late this evening. As far as Clifton Ewell is concerned I have not heard anything or any plans involving him. Jim all we can do is sit back and wait and let this terrible tragic thing play out. Jim as usual we are in a catch 22 and it's no way out but to leave or stay an play the Game. Peg we are not yet in a position to leave at this time but damn close we still have to stay a while longer.

Chapter 16

GHQM TRAGEDY

June 08,1939. Thursday afternoon GHVSP Prison Trustees Henry Johnson and Rubin James are pulling a Prison Food Wagon loaded with food trays from the kitchen out to the GHQM. After arriving at the mine entrance they load the food trays and coffee thermos bottles on to a Mine Rail Car. After they are through loading they both get in the car tightly fasten their seat belts and start their long two plus mile journey down to the "Big Lake Cavern" Branch and the Red Door Storage Area of the mine. Rubin tells Henry speed this fuckin Mine Rail Car up I am tired out and I want to get back to our Holding Cell so I can clean up and get some rest, it has been a long hot day. As they speed along they realize what a creepy place this cavern is and why the inmates assigned here call it the "Main Gate To Hell". Rubin so many people are living in death here. Murdered in Cold blood and listed as lost forever. Just Penitentiary Mystics. Henry are we not two of them, just a number waiting for our turn to happen? Henry all of us living within these GHVSP Dreary High Gray Prison Walls are just lost Souls. God Help Us?

As they approach the switch off that leads to the seldom used "Big Lake Cavern" Branch they slow down to make sure they switch over to the correct track. As they do this they strike a foul up in the track and the heavy Mine Rail Car takes a hard hit and almost jumps track. As luck would have it the car recovers and settles safely back on the rails. SOB, Rubin that was fuckin close had we jumped track we would have tumbled down that steep incline and rolled over in to the "Big Lake" and probably drowned. My God Henry that's the biggest fuckin lake I have ever seen in my life it must go on forever. Well you AH I have told you all about it many times. Yes, I know but your wild ass stories are so extreme at times I write them off as pure BS, HA, HA! It is now 1730Hr as Henry and Rubin finish checking the Mine Rail Car over and find very little damage. Satisfied its safe they climb back onboard and continue their journey. Henry lets go we are going to be all night delivering these fuckin food trays. Hell I can hear that fuckin bunch loading those Dynamite Boxes now, cussing out us two old niggers for being slow. Fuck them Rubin they are nothing but a bunch of white trash hunkies who think their shit don't stink.

As Henry accelerates the Mine Rail Car to hurry along, unbeknown to him the accelerator cables having been damaged in their accident at the switch off area are jammed. As he and Rubin look ahead they can see in the near distance the workers loading Dynamite Boxes from behind the open "Red Door" on too several Mine Rail Cars. All of a sudden Henry screams out, Rubin the brakes have been damaged and the accelerator is jammed I cannot stop this fuckin mine rail car we are going to crash!!!!!! Too little, too late as they collide in to the loaded

Mine Rail Cars at the Rail Track Block at the end of the line. An ignition takes place and all of the Dynamite Boxes are set off and begin to explode. The explosion within the "Big Lake Cavern" is so enormous the Cavern begins to collapse and crumble down within itself. The heavy pieces of Granite as it crashes in to the lake create a small Tsunami as the "Big Lake" floods over. These waters flood the entire Cavern and its branches throughout nothing goes untouched. God Help Us? The Green Heron Quarry Mine (GHQM) a. k. a. the Mine Gate to Hell (MGTH) crumbles down and becomes a Sealed Tomb, lost forever. God has finally destroyed this Den of Evil, TYDL. Is this another Penitentiary Mystic?

June 08, 1939. Thursday about 2100Hr the entire area of Carrisbrook is under somewhat of a siege as the huge explosions still continue to take place within the "Big Lake Cavern". Rescuer vehicles of all types begin to arrive on the site but for the Grace of God none are needed. The GHVSP although slightly damaged to some extent remains intact with no serious staff or inmate injuries but minor cuts and bruises and human shock. Back at Phills Pub GHVSP Chief Warden Foster also in slight shock cannot believe the extent of the tremors' as he like so many others suspected the tremors' were coming from a Major Earthquake. Finally the VASP issued radio broadcast and APB that the tremors' were being caused by a major explosion within the GHVSP GHQM. Those reports settled many folks down, TYDL. The Chief still at Phills Pub settles down and finishes his beer. He waits awhile for the traffic to subside a little then finally makes his way back to the GHVSP and his office. As he sits alone in his office he stares at the ceiling and sips on a glass of "Jackie Dee". He asks himself, what the hell happened, what the fuck went wrong? Who knows or will ever know? Jason what happened??????

Over in Carrisbrook, Peg and Jim sit together sipping on a cool glass of merlot wine. They too are in shock and also thought a Major Earthquake had occurred until the local radio station put out a news report speaking to the Mine Explosion at the GHQM just off of Lolly Dolly Road caused the Earth Tremors'. Peg looks at Jim and says what should we do? He tells her it's not much we can do and it's no since fighting the traffic and confusion to drive over there. Let's just relax sit here, sip another glass of merlot wine, listen to the radio news reports and take it easy. We can have a nice quiet supper go to bed early and just drive on in to work tomorrow morning as usual and get a report at that time.

June 09, 1939. Friday morning very early Jim and Peg arrive at the Chiefs and her GHVSP office. There sitting at his desk sound asleep with an empty "Jackie Dee" bottle is the Chief. Peg just lets him sleep as she puts on the coffee which she knows he will need. The smell of the coffee arouses the Chief as he wakes up and sees Peg and Jim sitting by her desk quietly chatting. Finally fully awake and settled Peg asks the Chief what happened? Peg I do not have a clue. All we can do is wait for the VASP Forensic Teams to investigate and file their reports and we all know that may take months. Peg for now I want you to call Assistant Warden Erma Kersay, newly appointed Assistant Warden Derrick Lamm and Security Force Captain Jason Mitchell to my office PDQ. All those called report to the Chiefs office except Jason. All sit saddened as rumors are flowing in that Jason may be one of those lost in the GHQM explosion. To clear the air the Chief states he is sure Jason was lost as he told me he would work late and be overseeing some Dynamite Loading work taking place in the GHQM. Folks until we receive all the reports from the VASP we cannot rely on rumors and speculate what took place, so all

I can say is business as usual. First order; Survey your sections and carry out a complete roll call and get that report back to me ASAP. Second order; Compile a list of notes about anything you may have heard, seen, or otherwise recall that may help us to complete and file a GHVSP report related to this Tragedy. That's it for now, any questions?

June 09, 1939. Friday about 1300Hr Peg and Jim are over at Phills Pub eating lunch. As you can imagine the place is packed with the local crowd and the conversations all speak to the GHQM Explosion Tragedy. Some of the very sad news within the Carrisbrook Community is the loss of Aubrey West Sr and his only son Aubrey West Jr. Both are well known honest business men that owned and operated one of the largest Mine Engineering Companies in the State of Virginia. Both are well known within their Church as very loyal and giving and will of course be sorely missed by family and friends. Jim and Peg sit and listen to this BS and laugh. Jim looks at Peg and says, honest and loyal my ass; both of those AH crooks would fuck a dead whore while they are stealing the pennies off of her eyes. As Peg and Jim continue to sit and just listen they hear Virginia State Rescue Workers and Teams that come and go speak to the severe damage to the GHQM they are seeing. Some speak to the debris and the many steel drums that have washed up from the "Big Lake" bottom that block the Cavern Branches. Peg looks at Jim and says; Holy Shit, if for some reason one of those drums should accidently be opened and human remains are found the shit is going to hit the fan around here big time.

June 09, 1939. Friday afternoon back in her office Peg as expected and as requested by the Chief, Receives and Scans the Roll Call reports the Staff has sent in. As she Scans the reports she lists the names of the missing as follows: GHVSP Staff Members; Captain Jason Mitchell and Sgt Clifton Ewell.

GHVSP Inmates; Henry Johnson, Rubin James, Vince Murphy, Guy Green, Blake Mason and Billy Pollock. GHVSP Outside Contractors; Aubrey West Sr and Aubrey West Jr. All other GHVSP Staff Members and Inmates are present and accounted for! Peg takes her completed list and places it on the Chiefs desk. As she does this she weeps and thinks what a terrible waste; all these men in their own ways caught up in crime and corruption. All entombed forever in the rubble of the "Big Lake Cavern". Dear God why do these things have to happen? Dear God Help Us, are Jim and I in our own way a part of this? I think so, like Jim said; we are in a catch 22 and it's no way out but to leave or stay and play the game.

Chapter 17

DOUGLAS LENTZ AND FRANK DALY LOCATED

July 07, 1939. Friday morning at exactly 0900Hr seated in the Chiefs Office are the GHVSP Special Five Members still remaining alive and well, they are; Assistant Warden Erma Kersay and Chief Warden Ken Foster. The only other living member and missing as usual is Virginia State Treasurer Wes Howard "The Big Man". The other two missing members are the late Charles Stanton and Jason Mitchell. Of course seated as usual, nonmembers Peg and Jim. The Chief opens the meeting as he speaks to the loss of Members Charles Stanton and Jason Mitchell. With some greedy enthusiasm in his speech he knows the GHVSP Slush Fund is now a three way split in lieu of five as this makes him very happy as his retirement is getting very close. The Chief looks over at Jim and asks him has he heard or gotten any notes from our outside friends? No Chief not yet, I am surprised as he looks over at Peg and casually winks. Peg knows what that wink means. Jim is there any other GHVSP final reports you need to discuss with us? No sir, all the State required Books are in perfect order and we should not have any problems with the State Auditors. Great let's make sure we keep things that way and of course separate. No problem Chief, no worry. Well that's all that I have does anyone have any questions at this time? If not this meeting is complete. The next Quarterly Meeting will be held sometime in October, Peg will schedule that as usual and let you know the date. As Jim leaves he whispers to Peg, let's go to lunch, now! Damn Jim it is only 1030Hr. Yes I realize that but there is something I need to discuss with you now? OK, let me get a few things squared away here real quick and I will meet you at the car about 1100Hr.

July 07, 1939. Friday about 1115Hr Jim and Peg are driving down Lolly Dolly Road as he hands her a note. Peg read this I just received it this morning in my Blue Bird House pick up box. Peg reads the note, it reads; Nice work and quickly planned, it has all been confirmed we will be sending you $300K. We understand and see your planned explosion in the "Big Lake Cavern" got out of hand somehow but many things do not go as planned or expected. With the "Big Lake Cavern" and your "SHE" escape route now destroyed, please work on another GHVSP escape route ASAP we are going to need it very soon. Jim that is a lot of money! I know! Are you going to show this note to the Chief? Hell no fuck the greedy bastard I have other plans in mind that I will report to him. As Jim pulls up to Phills Pub and parks he tell Peg let's go inside and get an isolated booth and I will review those other plans with you. Now inside quietly sipping on a cold beer in a back isolated booth. Peg is about to shit in her pants as Jim starts to tell her what he plans to tell the Chief. Peg this is what I plan on doing and I want to make sure it sounds convincing so give me any input you can think of? Peg here is the note I plan to give the Chief that I put together this morning at home. Read it and let me know what you think? The note reads; Your Planned accidental drowning of Prison Trustees Henry Johnson and Rubin James did not take place as described. VASP reports say they were killed in the GHQM Explosion Tragedy. No Gratuity! Peg that's it. Jim he is going to shit. Fuck him what can he do, hell he has no one he can run to and complain too. Jim what about the note you sent the Carbone Mafia Cartel speaking to the planned drowning of Johnson and James? Peg I never sent them that note, the only note I sent the Carbone Mafia Cartel I just quickly put together myself and sent later and it speaks to the GHQM Explosion as if we had planned it. The Carbone Mafia Cartel thinks we planned that so called successful GHQM Explosion that included the two insiders Prison Trustees Henry Johnson and Rubin James and the one outsider Security Force Guard Clifton Ewell that helped Doug Lentz and Frank Daly escape. The Mafia Cartel got what they ask for and was willing to pay for, all three escape helpers have been eliminated done deal. Peg we receive $300K in cash and no one knows about it but you and me. Peg what do you think? I think my little Jimmy is a fuckin genius!!!!!!

July 10, 1939. Monday morning about 0800Hr the Chief walks in to his office and sits quietly at his desk. Peg says Chief you are very quiet this morning what's on your mind has the cat got your tongue? No not really I am just a little concerned about all that debris and those steel drums the Virginia State Rescue Workers have found in the GHQM blocking so many of the Caverns Branches. Chief I would not be too concerned as I understand they have only collected twelve very old rusty drums and are transporting them to the nearby Carrisbrook Land Fill to be buried as we speak, no worry Chief. Peg I hope you are correct? By the way Chief this unopened confidential envelope addressed to you was in the mail box this morning. The Chief carefully opens the envelope and reads the enclosed note. Peg knowing what the note says and knows it is all BS from Jim just sits, watches and waits. As expected the Chief slams the note down on his desk and shouts; those no good tight fuckin bastards. Out of all the things I have done for them, this is how they treat and repay me! Fuck them, two can play this fuckin game. Peg call Jim and get his ass in here now. Peg calls Jim to the Chiefs office and as she hangs up she whispers; Jim be careful he just read the note and he is one mad SOB! Jim comes to the Chiefs office right away and walks right in. Here Jim read this shit? What do you think? Chief what can I think I really have no say so in these transactions they are planned by you and others, I am not a player. Well, what should I do? Chief knowing these Mafia people there is nothing you can do, they control you and this GHVSP. When the Fox Guards the hen house you play ball with the Fox. Chief just calm down and write it off. Jim I suppose you are right there is nothing I can do. SOB, Jim I sure would like to get my fuckin hands on that Local Carbone Mafia Cartel "Don", Harrison Paul Daly. Chief you and the VSBI and the FBI. No worry Chief one of these days someone will get his ass he is not bulletproof.

 July 10, 1939. Monday morning about 1000Hr in Biloxi Mississippi a beautiful black Cadillac car pulls up and parks in front of the newly established "Browning Nite Club & Game Room". Three men get out and walk in the side door of the Club unannounced and are escorted directly to Mr. William "Bill" Browning's private office. Two of the men sit down and wait outside. The lone man that is let in is none other than Harrison Paul Daly the Hampton Roads, Virginia Local Carbone Mafia Cartel "Don". SOB, Paul you finally got down here, nice to see your rusty old ass again I have been expecting you. Nice to see you Bill we go back along ways. Tell me about it, do we ever? Hell Paul I know why you are here so we can start your Carbone Mafia Review of this new Club anytime you feel like it. Well Bill, I am in no hurry as I always like to mix business with pleasure especially when old friends are involved. Not only that all reports from the New York City Carbone's indicate you are well up to speed with all the local City and State support you need. Yes Paul most of these local City and State officials we need are well paid and in place and things are running smooth like clockwork. We did have a few major problems getting started but I had those taken care of in a hurry although it did require a few more Boat Rides in the Gulf of Mexico than I expected. Damn Bill what was the problem? Paul to make a long story short doing these times of "Prohibition" and the State of Mississippi already being "Dry" we kept having Liquor Supply problems for our newly opened Club. To operate and stay in business we could not allow this. The Local Sheriff would not except our plans and our generous gratuity offers however he was reluctant but did except one of our Boat Rides out on the Gulf. The new replacement Sheriff was easy, no more problems! Anyway I have our Liquor Problems all settled. How did you swing that? No problem Paul! We receive three truckloads of assorted Booze each month from New Orleans, Louisiana. Two of these trucks drive through a special check point at the State Line and are cleared to pass, no questions. However truck three is stopped and retained by the local Sheriff's Office as a gratuity payment to supply other clubs here in town as needed. Paul a win, win situation for everyone. SOB, Bill Great Work!!! Hell Paul as far as the Club and Restaurant go we offer the prettiest and best strippers in the state and our food and serving sizes are second to none. Profits for the Carbone Mafia Cartel are well above expectations. Bill what you are telling me all sounds great but you know they want me to check out your Gaming and Gambling Room and Operation, that's where the big money comes from. Yes sir does it ever! Well let's do this; get you and your two Soldiers checked in then continue to walk around and let you see our beautiful Club, Beach front and small Boat Mariner. After that you can get some rest and plan on checking out the Gaming and Gambling Room Operations later when they fully open at 1800Hr tonight. Test times show our big profits occur between 1800Hr and 0200Hr. Sounds great lets go.

July 10, 1939. Monday afternoon Bill Browning escorts Paul to his Club Suite. Now all checked in Paul tells Bill you have a Beautiful Place here and a smooth operation and I am sure when I report all this back to the head Carbone folks in New York City they will be very pleased. Hell Bill you just might be looking at a promotion from a "Capo" to a "Don". SOB Paul, that would be great let's drink one to that, thank you. Well Paul let me run, if you need anything press the bedside button. I will come back around 1730Hr and take you to supper and show you our Game Rooms. I think you are going to be very surprised at how smoothly they operate.

July 10, 1939. Monday evening about 1745Hr Bill Browning and Paul Daly are seated at a very private table in the elite Club Gaming room. As they sit down unnoticed they order a nice "Jackie Dee" and chat. As they chat Paul says; Bill I saw in your Room Suites a Club Number you can buzz if you would like to have some female companionship provided. Yes indeed we found out early that these wild ass Southern Boys are crazy about Beer, Broads and Pussy (BB&P). That added service brings in a nice additional profit and we never have a shortage of beautiful girls, the line to get in is a mile long. SOB Bill a nice feature! Hell Paul later on tonight press the button, a little Pie at the "Y" might be something an old fucker like needs. Shit Paul try it out, get your old peg greased. Very funny Bill if anything it might kill an old man like me. Hell at my age "sex" is a number between five and seven, HA, HA! As Paul looks around he is overwhelmed with the Beautiful Game Room, the service and the smooth operation. It's only 1845Hr and the place is packed with all age groups. All Happy just having a few drinks, gambling and having a good time. It's hard to believe the place is jumping like this on a Monday night. Shit Paul you ought to be here on Friday and Saturday nights you can hardly get in the fuckin door.

As Bill and Paul sit chat and enjoy their drinks as old friends that go back along ways; Paul all of a sudden gets upset and gets a serious look on his face and then also uses his hand to cover his face. Bill seeing this asks Paul what in the hell is wrong you look like you have seen a ghost? Bill those two men on the game board stage handling the racing odds and numbers how long have they been employed by you? Paul I am not sure I guess from about early June, they are two of my best numbers men Patrick Payne and Russell Rice, do you know them? Do I know them you can bet your sweet ass I do, let's get the hell out of here. Bill Let's go back to my Suite and discuss those two they are big time trouble makers.

Back in Paul's Suite Bill pours them a big Jackie Dee over rocks as he now in a nervous state himself sits down to discuss Patrick Payne and Russell Rice with Paul. Bill the first thing I am going to do you may not like and I do not want to pull rank on an old friend but you realize you must comply. I understand Paul you being a Mafia "Don" whatever to tell me to do I will see that it is done and taken care of. Tonight when Patrick Payne and Russell Rice get off from work I want them eliminated, placed in steel drums and taken out in the Gulf and dumped overboard, PDQ, no questions asked. Holy Shit Paul are you kidding me? Paul how well do you know these two guys? Bill, Patrick Payne is my nephew, Doug Lentz and Russell Rice is my youngest son, Frank Daly. Paul what in the World have they done to deserve this tragic take down "Hit". You actually want family blood members eliminated? Bill it's along sad story so get us another Jackie Dee and listen up you will not believe what I am going to tell you about those two. It is now about 2100Hr as Paul finishes telling Bill about Doug and Frank. Bill just shakes he head. Paul I am so sorry and I fully understand you position. Bill I am very sad but these two killers have nothing to lose and they realize the Carbone Mafia Cartel wants them eliminated ASAP. They are both well armed and will kill you and me on the spot and not blink an eye. They are here for their own personal gain and safety with the old adage if you cannot defeat your adversary you join and conceal yourself within. Bill it's now 2130Hr I will just stay put here in my Suite as a safety measure, you go and set up the necessary elimination plans for Doug Lentz and Frank Daly as I told you too. No problems Paul it will be carried out as I am very familiar with the Mafia Laws and Codes. Bill I will say good bye at this time as I plan on leaving early in the morning. My Carbone Mafia Cartel Report on their new Club operation here in Biloxi as controlled by you will be rated excellent in all categories and it will include a section stating you and I located Doug Lentz and Frank Daly and their issued elimination requests have been carried out. Bill Browning I am sure after they review and verify my report you will be Commissioned as a Carbone Mafia Cartel "Don" in the coming months. Thank you Paul for your support and it's so sad to say good bye under these tragic circumstances but life is what it is and must go on. Paul I will pray for your family this

Sunday at early Mass, I will never forget you my friend, please come back soon, good bye! Thank you Bill, good bye!

July 11,1939. Tuesday morning about 0630Hr Harrison Paul Daly sits in his beautiful black Cadillac Car, his driver and bodyguard sit quietly up front. All three look across Rt 90, Biloxi Boulevard towards the Browning Nite Club Beach and small Boat Mariner and watch the beautiful Gulf of Mexico Sunrise. As they continue to watch they see two men load two steel drums on to the deck of a new Chesapeake Bay Dead Rise work boat (Mississippi State Marine Registration Number, MS 201HC. The name painted on the boat transom is "The Green Heron") and head on out to sea. Is this another Penitentiary Mystic? Harrison Paul Daly with tears streaming down his old worn face lightly whispers; Dear God Help me and Forgive me for what I do? He taps his driver on the shoulder and says; Allen let's go home to Norfolk, Virginia I have seen enough of Biloxi Mississippi to last me for a while. Maybe when we return for the wedding in November conditions will be Happy and we can let the sadness and this day be a thing of the past!!!!!!

Chapter 18

THE SECRET OF THE STEEL DRUMS

July 12, 1939. Wednesday morning about 0800Hr Peg is sitting at her desk in the Chiefs office reviewing her daily logs when the telephone rings. Hello! Peg this is the Chief I have made other plans and will not be in the office today. No problem Chief I will see you tomorrow is everything alright? Yes, no problems I will see you tomorrow have a nice day. As Peg hangs up she thinks to herself that was strange and the Chief sounded a little upset. With all the rumors about the GHQM accident tragedy floating around especially the finding of those old rusty steel drums that washed up from the bottom of the "Big Lake" the Chief has a lot on his mind. As Peg continues her work she hears a knock on the door and shouts come on in it's unlocked. She is surprised as it is the new Security Force Captain Lin Self.

Hi Lin, come on in grab a cup of coffee and let's chat a while, what's on your mind? Peg have you seen this, it's a Brief I just received from the VSBI? No, I do not believe so we have not received our copy yet. Well Peg I can tell you this the Chief is going to be very upset when he reads it. Here read it and make yourself a copy. Peg quickly reads the Brief, Holy Shit! The Brief reads; County Workers at the Carrisbrook Town Dump and Land Fill when burying old steel drums recovered and removed from the "Big Lake Cavern" GHQM Accident and Explosion Site; said one of the drums when it fell, accidently opened. As it tumbled and rolled it emptied itself of gravel and exposed the gruesome remains of a human body. Is this just another Penitentiary Mystic. As required by Law the Land Fill Workers right away stopped and called in a VSBI Forensic Team. This VSBI Forensic Team opened the other eleven drums on site and sadly found human remains in all of them. A full VSBI Rusty Drum Report is forth coming. VSBI Director Guy Chapman stated in the Brief that the human remains are in very advanced stages of decay and that positive identification may never be made. Peg looks at Lin and shakes her head and says; Lin you better take cover the shit has hit the fan big time. As Lin leaves Jim comes walking in to see the Chief. Jim he is not in today. Well what I was going to discuss with him can wait. Jim, Lin just brought this VSBI Brief in you need to sit down and read it! Holy Shit Peg, once this is fully investigated and a completed VSBI Report is filed some important heads around here are going to roll. The Walls of GHVSP will come Tumbling Down.

July 13, 1939. Thursday morning about 0800Hr Peg is at her desk sitting in a very nervous state as she realizes what is instore when the Chief arrives and reads this VSBI Rusty Drum Brief. About 0830Hr the Chief comes walking in. Good morning Peg how did things go yesterday? Well OK but we received this very disturbing Brief from the VSBI. We did what is it all about? As she gets the Chief a cup of hot coffee she says you better sit back and read it as she hands it to him. He laughs and says; no worry

Peg I have already seen this, our copy came late Tuesday after you and Jim had already left. I took it home with me, I have our copy right here. SOB Chief, for something this serious and disturbing you do not seem to be at all upset? Peg I am not upset at all, I took care of this Brief problem yesterday in my Lawyers Office. Whatever comes out of this completed VSBI Full Rusty Drum Report will not involve the GHVSP in anyway. How can you know this? Well let me explain to you what took place and was discussed in my lawyers office yesterday. First of all my Lawyer is Jacob Hempsville a well known Statewide Crimminal Defense Lawyer. His distinguished record shows he has never lost a case and fronts for the Carbone Mafia Cartel throughout the State of Virginia. To put it bluntly he has all his irons in the fire and all the bases covered. Well Peg as you know long before the GHVSP was built this property was owned and mined by the Dolly Family who still own and operate other Granite Mines in the State as we speak. Back then Mr. Dolly was ruthless and had a cruel reputation and it's been rumored miners that worked for him that he considered trouble makers for some reason or another were taken care of and soon disappeared. These rumors say that those poor souls were murdered placed in steel drums and dumped in the "Big Lake". Done Deal! My Lawyer tells me that since all of these drums are old and rusty and the human remains decayed to the point they cannot be identified he can prove all twelve drums were disposed of doing the Dolly Family timeframe. Peg he said with his friends in High and Low places he can make this happen to a degree that the GHVSP will not even become a player. SOB, Chief this Guy Jacob Hempsville is a genius. Chief I feel so much better and so relieved. Well Peg, keep what I just told you between you and me and of course Jim when you tell him tonight while you are sitting on his face, HA, HA! Shit Peg, pour us a Jackie Dee what the Hell. Chief I do not drink on the job, but I think it's time, like you said Chief what the Hell!!!!!!! I am so relieved!

July 13, 1939. Thursday evening as they drive home from work Peg all relaxed and relieved now that the VSBI Rusty Drum problem has been put to bed tells Jim what the Chief told her. Jim now also relieved tells her, SOB Peg that's a load off my mind also. It's been on my mind all day, just the thought of being arrested for some reason or having to appear in a Court Room Hearing was bugging the hell out of me. Hell Peg, we know from facts not rumors that there are steel drums on the bottom of the "Big Lake" that contain GHVSP Escapees that died in so called reported accidents. More Penitentiary Mystics. Shit let's forget about it and go home drink some merlot wine and eat some sharp cheese it's all now in the past.

July 24, 1939. Monday morning things seem to have settled down as the atmosphere around the GHVSP is back to normal conditions. With the loss of the GHQM there is no interior mine work and most of the GHVSP inmates are now assigned to exterior surface mine work, crushing gravel and working on roadways or just general building upkeep. Very satisfied with the way things have settled down and worked out the Chief knows he got lucky and dodged a few close calls. As he sits at his desk believe it or not he is very sad as he thinks about the loss of his close friends; Jason Mitchell, Clifton Ewell, Patrick Payne, Russell Rice, Charles Stanton and Roy Runyon. All these guy's had been onboard with him since the GHVSP opened for business back in April 04, 1933. All of these guy's in their own way died in the line of Duty. As he sits he reaches over and turns on his old radio scanner. As usual it pops and squarks as he listens to a few weak APB broadcasts, one still speaks to the Charles Stanton and Roy Runyon disappearance back on May 31, 1939. He wonders will they ever be found or will Doug

Lentz and Frank Daly ever be captured? Well let me get off my ass and play the roll and go and find someone's ass to chew on, Peg I will see you later.

July 24, 1939. Monday about 1200Hr Jim comes into the Chiefs office and tells Peg it's time to go to lunch! OK Hon, as she grabs her purse let's go! At Phills Pub they sit quietly and sip on a cold beer and chat. Here Peg look at this as he hands her a note he just received in his Blue Bird House pick up box. Peg quickly reads the note, it reads; check out the package I just placed on your work bench in your garage when you get home tonight! By the way "It's Time", think about it! By the way as a side note; Doug Lentz and Frank Daly just met their maker and took a Steel Drum ride out on the Beautiful Gulf of Mexico paid for in full by the Carbone Mafia Cartel. SOB Jim, who keeps leaving you these notes? Peg I rather not say at this time, I will tell you later. Let's just say I have friends in Low and High Places. What does this friend mean when he states "It's Time"? Peg let me settle a few more loose ends in the next several days and I will tell you what all of this means. Jim are you planning to tell the Chief about Lentz and Daly? Hell no, he would want to know my source of information. Hell he will find out later on when he realizes his own greedy ass is on very thin ice. Jim what are you telling me, I am completely lost what does all this BS mean? Peg like I just told you give me a few more days and I will tell you what it all means. Jim you are beginning to piss me off if you want pie at the "Y" tonight you better just rely on Minnie Fingers I am very upset and do not appreciate all these fuckin Secrets you have and keep from me!!!!!!

July 24, 1939. Monday afternoon Peg and Jim quietly drive home after getting off from work. Peg is still a little pissed off but has cooled down some as she does not want to interfere in Jim's plans and realizes he has a lot on him. Both are anxious to get home and check out the package his friend in Low Places left them. Jim pulls the car in the driveway hits the garage door opener and as the door opens he drives right on in. They both look and sure enough there sitting on the work bench is a beautiful wrapped package. Peg quickly but carefully opens the package. SOB Jim, would you look at this? A note on the box reads; $300K in crisp new $1000 Treasury Bills. (See Foot Note 4.). Good Luck, B.T. Peg is beside herself. Jim I do not know what to say! My dear do not say anything, let's go in relax have a cold glass of merlot wine and fix supper. As they sit and chat Peg asks Jim who is B.T.? Peg he is an old friend in Low Places you will meet real soon. Peg leans over and gives Jim a big kiss and whispers, little Jimmy will get his peg greased later tonight. Jim just laughs and says $300K will buy a lot of Pie at the "Y" and pecker grease that's for damn sure!!!!!!!!

Chapter 19

A SURPRISE AND SHOCKING CONCLUSION

August 18, 1939. Friday afternoon Peg has put all things in order around her desk and the office. She goes over a few loose ends with the Chief that he will need to take care of while she is gone especially her daily schedule and weekly logs. SOB Peg, I am going to be completely lost while you are gone this is the longest vacation you and Jim have ever taken. Most of your past vacations have been long weekends or just a day or so at a time. Hell Chief, no worry I will be back on September 04, 1939 Monday morning before you know it. If things get to be to much for you to handle call Erma from time to time to give you a helping hand. Peg I may have to do that! By the way where are you and Jim going? Well our plans right now call for us to drive up to Niagara Falls, New York then on up in to Canada. Well good luck, drive safe and I will keep the home fires burning. Thank you Chief take care of yourself and I will see you in about two weeks. The Chief gives Peg a big friendly hug as she leaves. Peg pats herself on the back as she leaves and thinks, that was a pretty good snow job I just put on the Chief.

August 19, 1939. Saturday morning about 0900Hr Peg and Jim clean up the kitchen, dress casually and go out and get in to their already packed up car. They slowly drive off to take what most family members and friends think is a two week planned vacation up North. What most of these people do not know is that it's a permanent full time move South to their newly purchased Condo in Panama City Beach Florida over looking the beautiful Gulf of Mexico. As they drive along Peg already having second thoughts looks over at Jim and says Hon I sure hope we are doing the right thing by making this move? Peg like my friend in Low Places said "It's Time". If he is correct and I know he is and all my last minute plans fall in to place as expected the wheels are going to roll completely off the GHVSP very soon and like I said Peg the walls will come tumbling down. Well, one thing for sure we will have no problems surviving and living high on the hog with our $300K nest egg that's for damn sure. Peg my dear I have more good news for you! You do? Yes our finances are much better than that and better than you think, I will explain this to you later. For now let me explain my plans for us I have been setting up and keeping from you for obvious reasons.

Well, for the past six plus years since the GHVSP Special Five was secretly and illegally put in to place by its five greedy members; Chief Warden Ken Foster, Assistant Wardens Jason Mitchell and Erma Kersay, Security Force Captain Charles Stanton and Virginia Treasurer Wesley Howard "The Big Man" to embezzle (Steal) GHVSP Funds I have handled and controlled their infamous GHVSP Slush Fund Book. Based on the Chiefs orders I have kept this book secret. The GHVSP Financial Book I maintain as required by the State for their yearly review is of course not secret and a separate public document. No problems. The only two people that even know about this Slush Fund Book and its location is the Chief and me. If by any accident the Slush Fund Book and its location is discovered it is to be destroyed by me or the Chief PDQ. Peg before we left work on August 18, 1939. I sent this Slush Fund Book to the Virginia State Attorney's Office by Special Carrier telling them the complete story involving this book that includes Planned Escapes, Mafia Gratuities, Mine Product Skimming and Inmate Salary Shake Down Taxes just to name a few. I can assure you, after they review this book and the VSBI investigates the people involved, the remaining GHVSP Special Five members still a live will be arrested and incarcerated for years to come, they are of course Chief Foster, Warden Kersay and State Treasurer Howard. Jim what about you and me will we be arrested or charged for our known noninvolvement positions. No I discussed this with the State Attorney before I even sent him the Slush Fund Book. He assured me we would be exonerated for finally coming forward and realizing we have received no financial gains and were forced players because of our GHVSP job positions. No worry my dear he promised me they will send us papers signed and sealed showing full vindication.

August 19, 1939. Saturday as Jim and Peg drive along on Rt No. 17 heading for their new Florida home they continue to chat. Jim you said earlier you had some more good news for me? He laughs out loud and reaches in his pocket and brings out a small box that contains a beautiful engagement ring and takes Peg's hand and slips the ring on. Miss. Peggy Vinsen, I love you very much will you marry me and move to our new home in Panama City Beach with me. She screams and tells him yes you big AH you know I will, "It's Time"! Jim I can tell you this that's enough good news for now, I am ready for a big glass of cold merlot wine. Peg let's wait a while before we stop for the night I still have some more good news you need to know about. Damn Hon, what can that possibly be about? Again Jim reaches in his pocket and hands Peg a Panama City Beach National Bank Book. Here Hon check this out and let me know what you think? Peg looks at the Bank Book and it lists the names of Mr. and Mrs. James Rawls Jr; Jim and Peggy Rawls. Tears of happiness run down Peg's beautiful face as all of this wonderful news at one time is just overwhelming her. Jim says, open the book and check out your bank account balance. Peg does this and screams holy shit Jim where did you get all this money to put in our account, it states two million dollars. Peg like I told you earlier I handled the GHVSP Special Five Slush Fund Book and each time I received Carbone Mafia Cartel Gratuity money I put aside one half of the amount I received for us. The reason I was able to do this I only reported to the Special Five Members one half of the amount received as expected payment to start with when it was actually double. As I paid the Special Five off every quarter in cash and I was the keeper of the book they would never know or care what the balance was to start with. If and when the Chief checked the book after each quarter the balance should and would always show Zero and the old balance would always equal the cash pay outs! Like my dad always said; naught times naught equals naught. Simple fuckin math!!!! All hidden and unknown to no one but you and me!

August 20, 1939. Sunday morning Peg and Jim are up early eating breakfast in a new Howard Johnson Motel and Restaurant just outside of Columbia, South Carolina. Well Hon how did you sleep? Hell Jim I was to wound up to sleep, all that wonderful news you presented to me just overwhelmed me. Well you better prepare yourself for more today because I am planning to drive straight through to our new Condo Home in Panama City Beach, Florida. Just wait until you see that place it is going to blow your mind. It's on the top level with a full balcony that overlooks the Gulf of Mexico. It's gorgeous and the view is breath taking. Sunday evening late Jim finally pulls up to their Gated Panama City Beach Condo, a neatly uniformed guard nods and says welcome home Mr. Rawls have a pleasant night. Peg is about to die with excitement as she cannot wait to go up and see her new home. As the elevator stops and the doors slide open Jim says there she is my dear, Condo No. 1201 straight across the hallway. As Jim unlocks and opens the Condo door Peg runs in and cannot believe her eyes. Jim it is beautiful and it's fully furnished with everything already in place. Yes my dear with all the latest whistles and bells. As Peg runs around like a chicken with its head cut off Jim is busy pouring merlot wine and cutting up sharp cheese as the doorbell rings. He wonders who can that be as no one knows they have moved but his Mom and Dad and his two other old friends in Low Places. Jim opens the door and a young uniformed usher hands him the daily local newspaper an tells him; sir you forgot to check your Newspaper and U. S. Mail Boxes down stairs in the Main Lobby. Sorry son we are new in town and I forgot. Yes sir, I know, no worry I will keep you straight and help you out until we get you potty trained, HA, HA! September 08, !939. Friday evening Peg still bubbling and Jim sit out on the balcony sipping merlot wine watching the Beautiful Gulf of Mexico. Jim laughs as he loves seeing Peg so relieved and Happy. As they sit Jim scans the Daily newspaper. SOB, on the second front page is an article that speaks to the Virginia State Treasurer Wesley Howard being arrested and charged with Embezzlement and Racketeering involving the GHVSP. As Jim continues to read, the article speaks to a VSBI Raid on the GHVSP as several key

Staff Members; Chief Warden Kenneth Foster and Assistant Warden Erma Kersay have been arrested and charged with similar crimes. Jim looks at Peg and says they finally got them! Jim what are you saying they finally got who? Wes, Ken and Erma have been arrested for skimming all that money over the years from the GHVSP Treasury Account. Peg I told you it would not take long, it's over. Peg I told you the only way we would ever get out of that catch 22 and no longer play the game was to leave. Hon, we did the right thing when we decided to get out of dodge and leave, TYDL.

September 15, 1939. Saturday afternoon about 1400Hr Peg and Jim are standing out on the Beautiful White Sandy Panama City Beach as they gaze out at the clear Blue Water and hold hands. A local Minister completes the wedding ceremony as he pronounces them Man and Wife. Four of their new neighbors and friends are in attendance as they all toast the newlyweds with you guessed it merlot wine. Well Hon we did it. Like my good friend in Low Places said, "It's Time"

September 18, 1939. Monday morning Jim is up early, he fixes himself a light breakfast of toast and coffee and decides to let Peg just sleep in. He goes down to the Main Lobby picks up the Local Daily newspaper and checks his U.S. Mail Box. Inside the Mail Box he is surprised to find two letters addressed to him one Post marked Norfolk, Virginia, the second Post marked Carrisbrook, Virginia. Back in his Condo and being very curious he quickly opens the envelope Post marked Norfolk, Virginia first and reads the letter inside. Holy Shit it reads; Jim, your friend GHVSP Chief Warden Ken Foster was found shot to death in his office, an apparent suicide. Jim stops and thinks to himself there is no way the Chief would ever kill himself just based on VSBI embezzlement charges. Something else must have taken place to set him off and make him do this. As Jim continues to read further he is shocked! It reads; On the Chiefs desk was found a final VSBI Report speaking to the "GHQM Rusty Drums". On one of the pages and underlined in "Red" the report states; "It has been confirmed that all twelve Rusty Drums contained unidentifiable human remains of murdered GHVSP Inmates. Confirmation of this was determined based on the fact that all of these bodies still had Prison Inmate anklet balls and chains attached". Jim puts the letter down and thinks, that super smart fuckin Lawyer Jacob Hempsville sure fell on his ass this time. I guess when he read that the human remains were so far advanced with decay and unidentifiable it was unnecessary to go and inspect them at the VASP Coroner's Office and Morgue in Richmond, Virginia. Hell Jacob, a stupid dumb ass ambulance chasing Lawyer would know to do this. Hell you AH you failed your client GHVSP Chief Ken Foster and let him down big time. The Chief, Ken Foster realizing he will now be arrested and charged with murder and found guilty and in all likelihood be sentenced to life without parole and would end up you know where? The dreaded GHVSP! No way could he take that chance; he just gave up and just threw in the towel and shot himself!!!!!

Jim continues to let Peg sleep as he pours himself another cup of coffee and opens the second letter from Carrisbrook, Virginia thinking it was from his parents he is shocked and laughs. SOB, it briefly reads; "Betty Daly (Flash Back; Betty Daly was engaged to VSBI Agent David Sikes at one time) and I are being married on Saturday November 04, 1939. The wedding will take place on the Browning Nite Club Beach at 1400Hr, casual dress. Jim our old friend, Sammy T. Jones will be my Best Man. You and Peggy better be there it's just up the road from your new Condo on Rt 90 in Biloxi, Mississippi. You and Peg will get to meet my future Father In Law, Harrison Paul Daly he is one hell of a nice guy. Signed your Life long friend Billy H. Thomas" B.T. Jim puts the letter down and laughs, how about that? SOB, I have not really socialized with Sam Or Bill since our old beer drinking, skinny dipping High School days at the "Butler and The Big Lakes". I wonder if they know our old "SHE" Big Lake escape tunnel was destroyed in that massive GHQM explosion?

Peg finally gets up. Well my new bride how did you sleep? Like a new born baby in a soft feathered bed. Hon, while I fix your breakfast and before you start reading the newspaper sit down sip your coffee and read these two letters we just received. As she reads the first letter from Norfolk, Virginia she is shocked but not surprised. Damn Jim I told the Chief I sure hoped his Lawyer had the "T s" crossed and the "I s" dotted, he said he was not worried, that all the bases were covered. All I can say is God Bless and Forgive Him! As Peg reads the second letter from Carrisbrook, Virginia she laughs looks at Jim and says it's a small World, I will put Betty Daly and Billy Thomas' wedding date on the calendar as we will be there with bells on that's for damn sure. Jim I know all of these people by name and have not ever seen or met any of them, that's strange. Jim how long has it really been since you have heard from Sammy or Billy? Not long Peg as they are two of my friends in Low and High Places. Both of them are Caporegimes Captains (Capos) working for the Local Carbone Mafia Cartel, their boss of course is "Mafia Don," Harrison Paul Daly. SOB Jim, you never told me any of this!!!!! Peg I never told you for obvious reasons, your safety and you never had a need to know; Peg as Paul H. would say, "Now You Know The Rest Of The Story"! Peg my dear the bacon is fried and the grits are hot buttered and ready, how would you like your eggs? Peg remember one thing my dear this World is not our Home we are just passing through so let the good times roll, TYDL!!!!!

Foot Notes

1. The Front Cover Picture. This picture is a Photograph of a Common Little Green Heron bird carving. This carving was designed and carved out of a block of Jelutong Wood by the Books Author John Jones. The Photograph was arranged and taken by the authors nephew Albert Gary Jones.
2. The Great Depression Time frame began in October 29, 1929 and spread worldwide until it came to a close in late 1939 or early 1941; no official date was ever recorded. It was the longest and most severe economic downturn in modern history. It was marked by steep declines in industrial production and price (deflation), mass unemployment, banking panics and sharp increase in notes of poverty and homelessness. Sad to say but many scholars say that World War Two brought the American economy out of this Great Depression. God Help Us, will it ever end? Remember "Greed" is a terrible thing and the root to all that is Evil!

3. The Civilian Conservation Corps (CCC) established in 1933 was one of the Federal Governments "New Deal" Programs. It was set in place to provide jobs for all levels of trades. The CCC stayed in place between November 03, 1933 and June 30, 1942 to stabilize the Great Depression.
4. The U.S Governmemt issued the first $1000 Bill in 1861. It was last printed in 1945 and due to lack of use taken out of circulation in1969. As of this day it is still legal tender.

Glossary

AH	Ass Hole.
a.k.a.	Also known as.
APB	All Points Bulletin.
ASAP	As soon as possible.
ASCS	Automatic Solitary Confinement Sentence.
BB & P	Beer, Broads & Pussy.
BS	Bull Shit.
Capos	Caporegime, Mafia Captain.
CCC	Civilian Conservation Corps. See Foot Note 3,
Co.	Company.
Don	Mafia Leader, The Boss.
e.g.	For example.
ETA	Estimated Time of Arrival.
etc	e - cetera.
FBI	Federal Bureau of Investigation.
GHVSP	Green Heron Virginia State Penitentiary.
GHQM	Green Heron Quarry Mine. (MGTH).
HC	Holding Cell.

Hr	Hundred hours.
i.e.	That is.
ISBN	International Standard Book Number.
Jr	Junior.
K	One thousand.
KP	Kitchen Police. Persons assigned to work in a kitchen.
Lt	Lieutenant.
MGTH	Main Gate To Hell. (The GHQM).
MS	Mississippi. (State).
NYC	New York City.
NY	New York State.
PAS	Piece a Shit.
PDQ	Pretty Damn Quick.
PE	Planet Earth.
POI	Persons of Interest.
POS	Piece of Shit.
PS	Post Script.
Qts	Quiet Side.
Sgt	Sergeant,
SHE	Satan & Hells Exit. (The GHVSP secret under water escape tunnel).
Snafu	Situation normal all fucked up.
SOB	Son of a Bitch.
Sr	Senior.
T/ CPA	Treasurer and Certified Public Accountant.
TNT	Trinitrotoluene. High Explosive Material.
TP	Telephone.
Triple "S"	Shit, Shower and Shave. (Military Slang).
TYDL	Thank You Dear Lord.
U.S.A.	United States of America.
VA	Virginia. (State).
VASP	Virginia State Police.

V.P.I.	Virginia Polytechnic Institute. A Virginia State University.
VSBI	Virginia State Bureau of Investigation.
WVA	West Virginia. (State).
WVSP	West Virginia State Police.

About The Author

John Jones was born and raised in Newport News, Virginia. He graduated from Warwick High School and later from William & Mary V. P.I. (Now Old Dominion University), Norfolk, Virginia. He retired after 42 years as a Marine Design Engineer and now lives in Brentwood, Tennessee.

CPSIA information can be obtained
at www.ICGtesting.com
Printed in the USA
BVHW042005270922
648084BV00018B/866/J